1.75

OR BE HE DEAD

OR BE HE DEAD

A Novel by

James Byrom

PERENNIAL LIBRARY
Harper & Row, Publishers
New York, Cambridge, Philadelphia, San Francisco
London, Mexico City, São Paulo, Sydney

This book was originally published in England by Chatto & Windus Ltd.
It is here reprinted by arrangement.

First PERENNIAL LIBRARY edition published 1982.

ISBN: 0-06-080585-4

82 83 84 85 10 9 8 7 6 5 4 3 2 1

CONTENTS

1 The Pulbury Shooting Case 7

2 How to Make Murder Pay 24

3 Yours Truly, Alfred J. Moxon 37

4 'There was an old war-horse called Shelley' 53

5 Foggy Romance 65

6 Mrs. Danby Lets the Cat out of the Bag 78

7 Getting Warm in Paris 95

8 Some Suicides Don't Like Heights 108

9 Progress in the Techniques of Love 120

10 'To Marcelline with love from Johnny' 131

11 La Futée 140

12 The Workings of 'Destiny' 150

13 The Cocktail Party 164

14 Millington-Forsett? 173

15 Pandora's Box 185

16 'Oh, my beloved pussies!' 198

TO JOAN

CHAPTER ONE

The Pulbury Shooting Case

At the time of the Munich crisis, a third collection of my essays about crime and criminals had just been seen through the press. The title-essay, *A Twist Somewhere*, was about a murder-case which had once been the talk of England. I had struck it, like oil, in the tundras of the British Museum newspaper store at Hendon: and the deeper I bored, the more enthusiastic I became, finding myself apparently first in the field. . . .

Today I walk with a stick and I have learnt that oil is inflammable. People point me out and say: 'There goes Raymond Kennington. I wouldn't have been in his shoes!' To which the cynics add: 'But you must admit he did pretty well for himself out of all that publicity!'

For reasons I shall mention, I like my villains to have 'pure' motives. And three of the gentlemen involved in the Pulbury Shooting Case formed a trio after my own heart. Without a bean to their aristocratic names, Millington-Forsett, Maningdon and Jermyn had taken a mansion and shooting in Sussex —complete with domestic staff and gamekeepers—for the winter season of 1894, each of them agreeing to pay a quarter share of the expenses. The fourth share was to be paid by a young guardsman called Sir George Richmond, who was rich enough to have paid the whole rent out of his own pocket. That was why he was asked to join the shooting party at Pulbury. And that was why, at ten o'clock one November morning, the owner's estate agent, Jack Travers, was mistaken for a pheasant by Claude Nevil Millington-Forsett.

That morning a party of five was walking through a wood,

trying to prevent some pheasants that had been driven into it by neighbouring sportsmen from escaping back over the boundary of the estate. The wood was thick and they were moving slowly through it in line when Millington-Forsett suddenly shouted 'MARK!' and fired into the undergrowth just ahead. A moment later the whole party was assembled gazing at the body of Jack Travers, who was lying on his face with the back of his head completely shattered.

Millington-Forsett seemed horrified by what he had done. But he was quick to point out that if Travers had not wandered out of line there would have been no accident. Though it was unusual to fire at a bird so low, the thickness of the cover, which prevented the 'guns' from seeing one another clearly, justified shooting at the birds as they rose, before they disappeared into the network of interlacing boughs.

At the inquest, the other members of the party all testified that though they had not seen the pheasant Millington-Forsett claimed to have shot at, they had heard flapping in the trees; which corroborated his story as far as possible in the circumstances.

The doctor was local, and so was the Coroner. Shooting accidents were not uncommon in those days of hammer-guns, and shooting tenants, especially when they came of the landed gentry themselves, were regarded as respectable people: they could hardly be suspected of murder. Verdict: Accidental Death.

Six months later Beresford Jermyn was arrested for blackmailing Sir George Richmond. Pressed by the police, with promises of a lighter sentence if he made a clean breast of the whole affair, Jermyn made no bones about incriminating Maningdon and Millington-Forsett. The latter, he said, had been the author of a scheme for relieving the baronet of his fortune, first by fleecing him at cards, and then, after allowing him to win back part of his losses, by formally accusing him of cheating. With three witnesses against him and his reputation as an officer and a gentleman at stake, they calculated that he would be forced to buy their silence and—what was more important—to go on buying it.

The project was put into execution two days after Travers's death. The baronet was duly accused of cheating and made to sign a document (Baccarat Scandal model) promising never to play cards again. Shortly after this the party broke up and the three conspirators regained London, leaving Sir George to pay all the expenses.

Two months later the blackmailing began. Millington-Forsett and Maningdon kept in the background. Somehow they had managed to make Jermyn responsible for collecting the money. So that when Richmond at last made up his mind to face the scandal and save what was left of his fortune, it was Jermyn who fell into the police trap, laid in a Soho public house.

Millington-Forsett and Maningdon had doubtless agreed on the story they would tell if Jermyn got caught: they completely denied Jermyn's accusations. They maintained that they had in fact seen Richmond cheating and swore that the document they had made him sign was the end of it as far as they were concerned. Millington-Forsett was even able to show that he had recently written to the baronet promising to pay his share of the rent—'as soon as my financial position improves'!

Faced with this cynicism, Jermyn had only one reply: he told what he knew of the Travers episode. It had been Travers's job to watch his employer's interests while helping the tenants make the most of the shooting. According to Jermyn, Travers soon began to have his suspicions about their solvency and good faith. At the very outset of their tenancy they had made the mistake of asking the agent to dine with them and talking too freely in their cups. One day, when the baronet was away on business in London, Travers was asked over to shoot. During lunch he disappeared for a time to settle a rent-dispute with a farmer. The conspirators were discussing their project in low tones so that the keeper, who was sitting not far away, could not hear what they were saying, when Travers suddenly reappeared, and his manner was so strange that they felt sure he must have overheard them. Jermyn was for calling the whole thing off and getting back to London at once, but Millington-Forsett insisted that the scheme still had a chance of success. 'You leave Travers to me,' he told them, 'I know how to talk to him.'

The police believed Jermyn's story, and though they could not collect enough evidence to put Millington-Forsett and Maningdon in the dock beside him on the blackmail charge, they went gunning for Millington-Forsett on a charge of murder. From the tangle of accusation and counter-accusation that ended in the sentence of Jermyn for blackmail, there emerged a preliminary sketch of one of the most sensational murder-trials of the century.

The case was heard by Mr. Justice Crewe at the Old Bailey and the court was packed with leaders of society, attracted partly by the personality of the accused, partly by his aristocratic connections. As an anonymous writer put it, reviewing the case in the *Gentleman's Own*—'the cold blue eyes, very wide apart, accepted the stares individually, making the gentlemen cough and jut their jaws, causing the ladies to blush and dip into their vanity bags. Most of the time the eyes were amused, even when they rested on the grave figure in scarlet enthroned beneath the Royal Arms. One had the impression less of a man on trial for his life than of a young blood in his box at the theatre in the last century, half absorbed by some coarse comedy of manners, half distracted by the fashionable throng.'

The characteristic poses of the prisoner were immortalized by Madame Morel, the principal artist of *The Illustrated*. Sometimes he sat back and twiddled his thumbs, sometimes he consulted his gold fob-watch. Occasionally he used his little jewelled pencil to scribble notes to his Counsel. But much of the time he was drawing sketches of the judge, the jury, and the celebrities in the well of the court. Even Madame Morel was caught by him, and among the illustrations on her page was the prisoner's impression of her sucking her pencil. He had passed it down to her during the final speech for the Prosecution.

The Prosecution groped its way into the heart of the case along a chain of suspicious circumstances—the renting of the shooting at Richmond's expense with promise of settling up later; Richmond's evidence, supported by Jermyn's, that he had falsely been accused of cheating as soon as he had started to win back his losses; and Jermyn's account of his conversation with Maningdon and the prisoner on the day before Travers's death.

"I do not hesitate to affirm," said Sir John Reilly in his final speech for the Crown, "that this conversation actually took place and at a moment of extraordinary significance. My learned friend will doubtless say that the only evidence we have for it is the word of a convicted blackmailer. The prisoner denies the whole thing, and so does Mr. Maningdon, who, if we are to believe his evidence, was the white-headed boy of the party. But Jermyn has already been dealt with by twelve just men, and I put it to you, Members of the Jury, that he is a far more credible witness than Maningdon or the prisoner. He has nothing to gain by telling a lie, and you may well agree with me in concluding that in telling the truth he has run a grave risk of being involved in a charge of murder. You have heard Jermyn say under oath that directly after the prisoner and his two confederates in the blackmail scheme suspected that Travers had overheard them plotting, the prisoner said, 'leave Travers to me, I know how to talk to him'. In view of what happened the very next morning, what possible construction can you put on those words but that he meant to kill Travers, and as expeditiously as possible. You may think, with me, that in these circumstances words would have less force than gunshot!

"I come now to the events of the morning of November 30th. It was a dark, slightly misty morning; unsuitable for shooting, one would have thought. The cover chosen for this morning's sport was thick and difficult to walk, and it was the prisoner, be it noted, and not the gamekeeper, who marshalled the 'guns' into line for the walk through this tenebrous wood. You have heard the gamekeeper state in evidence that this was unusual, though since the gentlemen wanted things that way he did not consider it his place to interfere. Now, where did the prisoner put Travers? The honest gamekeeper has told us that Travers was placed in the middle of the line, on the grounds that he knew the terrain well and would therefore be able to keep the line together. If we are to believe the prisoner's account of the shooting, Travers was not very successful at the task he had been given—he must have been ranging well ahead of the line, utterly lost in a wood he knew intimately! But why shouldn't Travers have been placed in the middle? Because—again we know it from the gamekeeper—the best position in that beat was outside the wood altogether, in an open field which afforded the only chance of a sporting shot at a pheasant. That was where Travers, as the only guest in the shooting party, might have been expected to be placed. Yet it was Sir George Richmond—this unfortunate young man who was never able to say 'no' to the prisoner—who was placed in this favoured position. Not, as you might think, to enable him to enjoy better sport—oh no! he was destined to *provide* sport—he was sent there because, apart from the keeper, he was the only member of the shooting party who would have dared to raise his voice against the prisoner. The others, so far as the killing of Travers was concerned, could be relied on to hold their tongues if they saw anything suspicious: a word from Millington-Forsett and they could have been involved in a conspiracy to murder.

"I turn now to the days that followed the shooting of Travers. For the survivors of that party they must have been depressing days, what with the inquest and the funeral. How do these gentlemen pass the time? Very properly they do not shoot any more, except to pot at rabbits from the drawing-room windows. They spend their time indoors, gambling. Sir George has told us very frankly that for his part he didn't approve of gambling so soon after the tragedy: but that having lost so much money already, he couldn't forgo the opportunity to win some of it back. One can understand Sir George. But you would have thought that the gentleman who had just killed his shooting guest would have been loth to give Sir George his chance so soon. But no! It was the prisoner who suggested to him that it was a great pity to stop playing just when his luck was beginning to turn. It was the prisoner, whose financial position was so precarious that he could have done with a little extra, if only to help him pay his share of the rent, who seemed positively anxious to relinquish his ill-gotten gains! . . . Could this have been due to a guilty conscience?"

Sir John Reilly piled on the irony in a brilliant attempt to win a case which, as he afterwards admitted, had seemed to him hopeless from the beginning. The police and the Director of Public Prosecutions had handled the affair clumsily. Far more serious from the Crown's point of view, rain had long obliterated all traces of foot-marks from the wood, and though it was still possible to find the exact spot where Travers had fallen, from pellets embedded in the trees, the medical experts disagreed with the gun-experts about the spot from which Millington-Forsett had fired. This conflict seriously weakened one of the main points in Sir John's argument: that if the undergrowth was too thick for Millington-Forsett to be aware that his victim was just ahead of him, it was also too thick to allow so many pellets to pass unhindered into Travers's skull. The Defence further weakened this part of the evidence by producing witnesses to demonstrate that in gun accidents the most extraordinary flukes were possible. And they severely shook Jermyn's evidence about the prisoner's share in the blackmail conspiracy by bringing a bookmaker into court to prove that Jermyn had a grudge against Millington-Forsett over an unpaid betting account. In the absence of proof that any part of the blackmail money had actually passed into Millington-Forsett's pocket, his motive for killing Travers could only be presumed. As for the crucial utterance 'leave Travers to me, I know how to talk to him'—even if he had actually said those words, it was possible to put different constructions upon them. According to Millington-Forsett's Counsel, who pronounced them in a very different way from Sir John Reilly, they could well have meant, 'I'll find out what Travers really knows—I speak the same language as he does.'

Millington-Forsett left the Old Bailey a free man. But it was noted by one of the journalists present that when he shook his defender's hand the eminent barrister did not smile or speak to him, and passed out of court with a curt nod.

My revaluation of this case contained one new piece of evidence. I had been over the ground with the son of the gamekeeper who accompanied the shooting-party and he told me for a fact that the bird at which Millington-Forsett claimed to have fired got up well behind his father and could not possibly have been in line with Travers.

"Why," I asked him, "did your father say nothing at the inquest?"

"Because Mr. Millington-Forsett was a gentleman, and it weren't his place to open his mouth."

"But later, at the trial, when he must have known the man was guilty, why didn't he speak out then?"

"Because our folk was always respectable, and my dad didn't want to get into trouble, having shut his mouth the first time, like."

Proof copies of *A Twist Somewhere* had already been circulated to the book-trade when a small bookseller called Pusey in Bedford wrote to Hodge and Ricketts and asked if they were aware that the last author to discuss the case in print had been successfully sued, with his publisher, to the tune of twenty thousand pounds.

Hodge and Ricketts were small publishers with a long tradition of good book-production and a reputation for taking risks on writers of high literary value but little immediate popular appeal. I was not one of those authors, but they cherished me as the missing link between their ideals and their livelihood. *Black Museum* had gone into five impressions, *Gloved Fingers* had achieved a popular edition, and *A*

Twist Somewhere was already heavily subscribed by the trade at the moment when the blow fell.

Mr. Hodge telephoned the news at once. "So there it is," he concluded, "and there's nothing we can do about it till we can get a legal opinion. In the meanwhile we're withdrawing every copy from circulation."

His tone, I thought, was slightly hostile, which didn't really surprise me in the circumstances. I could imagine him sitting at his desk in Temple Bar, staring at the grim façade of the Law Courts opposite as if he expected cannons to pry suddenly through the portage and blow his publishing house to smithereens. As the grandson of the founder of the firm he took pride in preserving the original atmosphere of the place. He approved of the Dickensian pokiness, the musty smell, and the general atmosphere of dilapidation, as a setting uniquely appropriate for the planning and editing of books. It was an *atelier*, he insisted, not an office; and he spoke of his employees, from the production manager right down to Betty, the girl who worked the telephone exchange and tied up parcels between calls, as 'craftsmen down to their fingertips'.

Three days later, in response to an urgent summons, I turned in under the sign of the Golden Eagle—the work, it was said, of G. F. Watts. As I climbed the creaking oak staircase I amused myself by drawing squiggles on the broad, dusty banisters. The first-floor landing gave on to the storeroom, Mr. Ricketts's room and the office of the production manager—at least it would have 'given', if it had not been blocked by parcels of books. Josephine Canning, Mr. Hodge's secretary, was climbing over them, trying to make a passage through to Mr. Ricketts's door. She leapt down as I arrived, and dabbed spit on a ladder in her stocking.

"It's all *your* fault," she said, with a charming glare, "*you're* responsible for this appalling bottleneck!"

"Oh come!" I said. "I don't see anything abnormal."

"Your brainchild"—she blew the dust off a shoulder-high stack—"all packed up ready to be launched on the world, and now this has to happen! Whether there's any just cause or impediment or not, it's all very upsetting. That jacket I designed was sensational. Mr. Hodge says it's better than the book!"

I looked at her sternly. She was wearing a kind of waistcoat, red with gold buttons. It went wonderfully with her fair hair and complexion.

"Did you design *that*?" I asked, pointing at her waistcoat. "I think *that's* sensational!"

"No I didn't," she said. "And now I think Mr. Hodge is waiting for you. He has a loaded revolver on his desk."

Hodge was a small grey man like a seal, with a wispy moustache, a harsh voice and sad, inward-looking eyes. His father, it was said, had forced him to go into the family firm when he wanted to become a musician. He had done several years in the publishing house, then after an appalling quarrel with his father, 'run away' to be a pianist. Several years of intense study, followed by a period of playing in provincial theatres and tea-time trios, finally disillusioned him, and he was reconciled to Hodge Senior only a year before the old man died. Ever since then he had felt guilty, and though Ricketts had joined the firm a few years before his father's death, injecting new capital and new ideas, Hodge wanted nothing better nowadays than to keep the firm as it had been in his father's day. Publishing less from vocation than posthumous filial piety, nothing really kindled him but poetry and the idea of educating the public in music: when discussing the rare musical books on his list he played five-finger exercises all over his desk and wanted to rewrite them all himself.

Today there was nothing to kindle him at all, but the thought that one of the moneymaking authors his partner had insisted on introducing was putting his beloved firm in jeopardy for some trumpery essay about a criminal everybody had completely forgotten.

"Well, Raymond," he said—it was a Hodge and Ricketts's convention to call all their authors by their Christian names, but he always made it sound like a convention—"as you can imagine, we're very worried about this business—we've never had anything like it before, not even in my grandfather's time when we did a scurrilous pamphlet by Whistler."

I said: "I treated the man as a historical character. It never occurred to me that a rogue like that could have survived, and I don't suppose it occurred to you either. What are you going to do about it?"

"What are *you* going to do about it? Here's the reply from Liversidge of the Temple. He says in effect that if Millington-Forsett is still alive—and that's possible if your dates are correct—the whole thing is tendentious and in the highest degree actionable. Having been acquitted of murder the law presumes him to be innocent, and he is entitled to its full protection." He handed the letter over the desk and while I glanced through it: "I've discussed the whole question with Ricketts and we agree that if Millington-Forsett is alive, there are only two possible courses: either you substitute another essay or you rewrite *A Twist Somewhere* under legal supervision . . ."

I was on the mat and I did not like it. Hodge managed to convey that he thought the whole business disreputable, a smutch on the firm's imprint.

"But that essay is the best thing in the book—my interview with the gamekeeper's son puts a new complexion on the case—I am relying on it to sell the book . . ."

"I know. Ricketts is most disturbed about that. But unfortunately we are not in a position to take the slightest risk of provoking an action. As it is we shall be let in for heavy expenses now that the book is set and the binding advanced."

"Then the first thing to do is to find out if Millington-Forsett is dead?"

"Exactly, and as quickly as possible. The book is on our Christmas list and if we wait until Spring it may go cold on us."

I ground my teeth and let that pass: "Then what do you suggest—a private detective agency?"

"Too expensive for us just now. Normally, of course, we would entrust Liversidge with the research. But there again, I'm afraid. . . . I say, Raymond, couldn't you do it yourself?" He relaxed a little and smiled with difficulty. "After all, it's right up your street, isn't it? And if the book ever goes into a second edition, you might be able to add a very interesting appendix!"

On the way out I met Josephine again. I had a wild idea that she had been lying in wait, for she popped out of a door just in front of me and went trickling down the stairs in her soft flat shoes like a stream of molten gold.

"Miss Canning!" I called out. "What's the hurry?"

"Oh, hullo!" She turned round innocently as I caught up with her on the street. "I thought you were Mr. Cutts. He's apt to pursue me at this hour hoping for a little *tête-à-tête* about printing costs. Actually I like reading over my lunch— one becomes so abysmally ignorant working in a publisher's!"

"Pity," I said, "I wanted to ask you to have lunch with me."

She appeared to hesitate for a moment.

"Well, if you promise not to talk about printing costs, I *think* I'd love to."

We walked slowly towards the Strand. I had asked her on impulse and now I was speechless at my own boldness. The more women attract me the more they intimidate me, and Josephine was suddenly formidable. The easy camaraderie of the office had become impossible now that I was alone with her in the street, jostled by the stream of office-workers hurrying away to their lunch.

"What about the Temple Bar Restaurant?"

"Oh not that, please. Mr. Hodge always lunches there, and there's always Archie Macdonnell and Beachcomber and half a dozen others who have to be admired and listened to."

"Then what about Gow's?"

"For God's sake! Mr. Ricketts always lunches there when he's taking one of his authors out."

"Simpson's then?"

"Too predominantly male. Besides I might meet my step-father entertaining his business friends. . . ." She gnawed her upper lip and looked at me thoughtfully. "I know a quiet Italian place in Holborn where you sit in plush loose-boxes and struggle with yards of spaghetti. Couldn't we take a taxi and go there?"

During the taxi-ride I was still speechless, and Josephine, wondering why on earth I had asked her, chattered gaily about books and authors, flitting from one to another with such bewildering superficiality that it was all too obvious she was only discarding in the hope of giving me the lead.

Finally, encouraged by *chianti* and the arrival of a dish of bubbling *gnocchi*, I hinted at my exasperation:

"And what would you have been reading if I hadn't had the nerve to ask you to lunch?"

From an outsize handbag she fished out a red volume with

the stamp of the London Library on it. She handed it to me in silence, watching my face eagerly. '*The Trial of Millington-Forsett*,' I read, 'Edited by James Lamont, Barrister-at-Law.'

"I was so fascinated by your essay," she said, "I simply had to read a full report of the trial. And now this libel crisis has turned up, the whole thing seems to have come to life. I feel as though I were involved myself."

"Would you like to be?"

"How do you mean?"

"Would you like to help me find out about Millington-Forsett?"

Her face lit up. She was no longer the society girl who had done her season and was filling in the time before marriage by dabbling in literature and the arts.

"Oh goodness!" she said, "I should be scared—I mean, thrilled to death! But you're not serious. Why should you ask *me*, of all people?"

I was wondering myself. It had been my second impulse in half an hour. But I have so few impulses that I am apt to believe in them.

"Because you have a reputation for being efficient—Hodge wouldn't have you otherwise, or would he?—and because, well, you're one of the family. This isn't a thing that should be spread about."

She stared at me for a moment, then said: "But you don't know anything about me. I'm a fool, an utter fool, and a frightful gossip. The whole story would be all over London in twenty-four hours!"

"Hodge wouldn't have you if you gossiped!"

"But that's different—that's work."

"This is work too. A great deal of Hodge and Ricketts's money is at stake and Hodge didn't conceal the fact that the firm's financial position is rocky at the moment."

"All right then. I'm on. But I think you're crazy all the same."

She put down her knife and fork, lit a cigarette, and looked from her glazing *gnocchi* to me: "I wonder what you're really like? Nobody in the firm knows anything about you except what you say in the blurbs. I know that by heart . . . 'a Londoner born and bred . . . interested in crime since his schooldays when he unmasked the thief of the Sports Challenge Cup . . . tried his hand at shoplifting to see how it would feel and very nearly got sent to prison, because the Manager, with whom the *coup* had been arranged, went on holiday without telling him . . . unmarried, in his late thirties . . . in between bouts of work, allows himself to drift without plan or direction until some situation or event brings him back to his writing desk . . .' It sounds fascinating, but there's terribly little to go on. I feel I'm entitled to know more!"

"But there isn't any more to know, that's why it sounds fascinating. Pick bits out of anyone's biography and you can build him up to be quite a figure. The truth in this case is mostly between the lines. I'm terribly lazy, I'm a frustrated novelist, and my drifting is mostly with my feet on the mantelpiece reading the *Police Gazette* and the *News of the World*. I'm the jackal behind the journalist, always at several removes from my subject. I like writing about criminals because they're ready-made characters. Just fill in a few human touches, generalize from habits of speech and appearance, add a spot of moral criticism, and you appeal to the potential criminal in all respectable people. They will always pay to find out where 'but for the grace of God' they might have landed up themselves. It was Ricketts who wrote that blurb, and the shop-lifting affair was only a publicity stunt suggested by a newspaper. . . ."

22

"You're modest anyway, so I'll let you off the more personal questions. Well now, what can I do about Millington-Forsett? Do you think he's still alive?"

"His type are apt to live long: they know how to look after themselves. Anyway, there are two preliminary enquiries that have got to be made before we try anything more complicated. The first port of call is Somerset House, though it's extremely unlikely that a man like that would be buried under his own name. If that's negative, try the Editor of the *Peerage and Baronetage*. If he's dead and his family know about it they might have thought it worth while adding a decent date to his career. On the other hand they might have refrained, for fear of letting loose people like me. Meanwhile, I'll find out from Pusey when this libel action was brought. If we know what he was doing at the time, we might get a clue as to what he's doing now. His age is too respectable for crime, but with a past like that he certainly doesn't call himself Millington-Forsett. . . ."

CHAPTER TWO

How to Make Murder Pay

As I listened to Pusey on the telephone I painted his portrait in my mind. I saw pince-nez on a sharp nose and short grizzled hair stretched on a backless, pedantic skull.

"Yes, yes," he rasped, "if you will wait a minute I have it all here. I am not surprised you found it expedient to ring me."

I could hear his breath whistling through his teeth and a dry rustling in the background. Then he cleared his throat with a noise like the tearing of calico. "Er . . . hullo? Mr. Kennington? The article that brought Millington-Forsett into the limelight again was published in *Whispers*, August, 1927. The author was J. T. Twight, a free-lance writer with a somewhat unenviable reputation for raking up scandals: the action was brought against him and Sunray Publications jointly. Like yourself, he had obviously not taken legal advice. His account of the case was far from objective as a whole and one sentence was singled out by the plaintiff as being particularly objectionable . . . let me see, ah yes, it was the concluding sentence in the article—'And so the Sussex woods still guard their dark mystery and Jack Travers sleeps in Wisborough Churchyard, in the sheltering shade of an ancient yew-tree.' . . . You are surprised? Ah, I thought so. Authors as a race are lamentably ignorant of the law, so perhaps you will allow me to point out to you what was objectionable about this sentence? You see, there was no 'dark mystery' in law, because Millington-Forsett had been tried and found innocent. To state that there was still a mystery was to suggest that the truth had not come out. To assert, further, that Jack Travers slept in the *shelter* of a yew-tree was to insinuate that in life he had been attacked. Mr. Millington-Forsett had no difficulty whatever in proving that he had been libelled, though as to the assessment of the damages the case was somewhat complicated by recriminations between the joint defendants. Have I made myself clear? Good. Oh by the way, Mr. Kennington, I have noted one or two spelling mistakes in the page proofs, doubtless overlooked by you in the rush to catch the Christmas market. Would you like me to send you a list of them?"

"Thank you, Mr. Pusey. But I think you can leave me and my publishers to worry about the spelling mistakes. We are already extremely indebted to you for saving us from the risk of an action . . . what? . . . yes, yes, I agree that the bookseller has a great public responsibility. Thank you, again, Mr. Pusey—you have indeed proved worthy of your profession. As an author I . . . yes, and on behalf of Hodge and Ricketts too . . . well goodbye, Mr. Pusey . . ."

Neither Sunray Publications nor *Whispers* appeared in any recent work of reference, but a telephone call to a friend in Fleet Street put me on to Bingham's Press, which had bought up Sunray Publications in 1930, allowing the shattered *Whispers* to 'sleep in the sheltering shade' of oblivion.

The building which housed this enormous publishing enterprise was a skyscraper by London standards, a great mass of ferro-concrete and glass, blazing, it seemed, with a thousand brilliant inspirations for saleable fictions and articles. I was regarded as a kind of saboteur who had had the misfortune to fall into the churning wheels and slow down the whole machine. I was thrown from one part of the building to another and might easily have been ejected with the waste paper if I had not stumbled, more by accident than judgement, on a fat, friendly man in a lavatory. When I mentioned

Sunray Publications his face was transfigured. He conducted me along a narrow passage to the editorial offices of Bingham's *Wild West Magazine for Boys*.

I could hardly believe my luck when he told me that his name was Patterson and that he had migrated from the defunct *Whispers* straight to his present job. "Same sort of racket," he said genially, "though you mightn't see the connection at once. Didn't myself, till the editor of this rag asked me if I knew anything about cattle rustlers! 'Well,' I said, 'I've been raking up muck about tattlers in bustles, so I reckon I'm qualified for making up truck about cattlers in rustles!'" He laughed, then stopped abruptly, wheezing: "Now tell me what you want to know about *Whispers*—you can't sue the dead, you know!"

My story was continually interrupted by the telephone and by a young woman called Liz, whom Patterson described with a leer as a 'comfortable bit of office furniture'. When I had finished he took off his glasses and polished them, staring at me with naked unfocussed eyes, which the powerful ceiling-light seemed to hurt. He said: "J. T. Twight was a nasty piece of work. But he had a flair for corpses worth exhuming. He gave my chief his solemn word of honour that that article had been passed by a lawyer."

"How could it have been?"

"Ah, that's just it. The lawyer was called as a witness for Sunray Publications and his evidence was that Twight must have changed the script after he had passed it. Twight claimed that he had never written the words complained of, that his article had been edited by us to make it more sensational. I gave evidence that it had been sent to press just as it stood. . . . Look here, old boy, you know as well as I do that Millington-Forsett is still too hot to touch. If I tell you what I think about that action, will you promise to treat it as confidential? . . . Very well, then. I think the whole action was a put-up job between J. T. Twight and Millington-Forsett to get money out of Sunray Publications. They picked on *Whispers* because it was a paper that was habitually in trouble and they reckoned the Courts were ready to pounce."

"How could it have been a put-up job? Didn't Twight have to pay up too?"

"He was an undischarged bankrupt at the time. Sunray Publications took the real rap. Now I'll give you a bit of information I've been keeping to myself for future use. Very late one night a few days after the libel action, I was walking down Jermyn Street when I heard laughter in the doorway of a Turkish Bath. I looked round, and, bless me, there was Twight leaning against a door with his arm round another man's shoulder. Though the lighting was bad, I am quite certain the other man was Millington-Forsett—I couldn't mistake that white wrinkled face, the little goatee beard and the air of old-fashioned distinction that so impressed everybody in court. I tell you, it gave me quite a turn to see those two laughing together—there may have been bad blood between them, but they were certainly the best of pals by then . . ."

I was fascinated. It had occurred to me that Millington-Forsett might have changed his spots in the quarter century between his acquittal and the Twight libel. In a way it was a relief to hear that far from being persecuted by the society he had outraged, he had been making money out of murder as recently as thirteen years ago.

"Mr. Patterson," I said. "You've done me a real service . . . now if only you could help me find Twight! . . ."

"Ah," he said, "now you *are* asking. Twight was fished out of the Seine a year after the libel action. There was a suicide letter and he had taken the precaution of predrowning himself in drink. He made headlines in the *Sunday Globe*, the newspaper he was writing for at the time."

"Was there any suspicion of foul play?"

"I don't think so. The letter was in his handwriting, the style was unmistakably bogus (which means it was genuine Twight), and apparently some girl had given him the bird. Anyway, the newspapers were all so scared of Millington-Forsett that they didn't even suggest the obvious connection between the suicide and the libel action. But if I remember rightly, it was the general feeling in Fleet Street that Millington-Forsett had struck the death-blow and the girl merely finished him off—figuratively speaking, of course!"

Patterson read my expression and laughed ghoulishly.

"Just think! If it hadn't been for Twight, *you* might have been the one to get it in the neck!"

I was dozing in my armchair about eleven when Mrs. Roddie called me to the telephone on the landing.

"You might tell your friends to ring airlier," she shouted up the stairs, "I was just putting on my nightshairt and I thought maybe you'd slipped out to the pub."

"I was dozing," I said peaceably. "Anyway, it might have been a call for you."

Mrs. Roddie made a winded noise as though somebody had punched her in the solar plexus. "You knew very well it wasn't for me. And if it's a sairvice flat you want. . . ." I didn't listen to the rest, I was listening to a voice saying 'this is me' in response to my rather gruff 'who?'

"Who's ME?" I repeated.

"Josephine Canning. What's the matter? Did I wake you up? Were you expecting somebody else to ring? Or have you got dyspepsia?"

"Yes, to the last question," I said. "That's my landlady's Christian name. Any news, Josephine?"

I don't use Christian names unless I'm forced to with people I don't know well. But this one came out spontaneously. It was my third impulse in one day and I suppose there was a second's hesitation in my voice before I gave in to it. At any rate her voice seemed to stiffen and become a shade more businesslike. "No real news. But I've got some facts that might interest you. Would you like it over the phone or would you rather wait?"

"I'd rather not have it over the phone—Dyspepsia may be listening. I'd rather not wait, either. I suppose you wouldn't come round here for a drink? It's late I know, but not too late to ruin your reputation."

She laughed: "That might have been better put, mightn't it? As a matter of fact I *could* come round—I'm so bad at thinking up excuses quickly. The chief snag to my mind is that you live in the slums of Pimlico, and though I'm not so worried about my reputation I don't want to be knocked on the head!"

"My district may be shabby," I said, "but I'll have you know that it's perfectly genteel. Now just get into a taxi, and if you tell him to drive along the embankment there's no need for you to defile your eyes with Lupus Street. . . ."

When I hung up Mrs. Roddie was standing below in her nightsark, a formidable rectangular apparition cut into sections by the banisters.

"Mr. Kennington," she was saying, "I'll thank you to keep a civil tongue in your head. I haird every worrd you were saying and if you think you can stand there and insult me, I'll remind you that this is my house and there's *gentlemen* coming every day to ask if I've a room to let. There's others in this street taking four pound a week for the comfort you're enjoying for three. . . ."

"Now, Mrs. Roddie! You know very well I was only teasing you. I haven't any secrets from you, and I don't care a damn if you *do* listen to my telephone conversations. . . ."

"I wasn't listening. I just couldn't help hearing: and it's a good thing too, for this house has a good name and I'll thank you to remember that as far as the neighbours are concairned, any woman whatever—be she a duchess or a bishop's lady—is just a *feemul* after twelve o'clock!"

"The neighbours are old cats and I'm surprised at an intelligent woman like you taking any notice of what they say. In fact, I should be *black-affronted* if I didn't know that you always mean well. But of course, if you really would prefer to get another lodger . . ."

"I never said anything of the kind. Goodnight, Mr. Kennington. The bacon's a wee bit salt today, so you'll just have to do with an egg to your breakfast."

When I heard Josephine's taxi arrive I went down and let her in. She had come almost straight from the theatre and as she took off her fur and settled down in my threadbare armchair I was momentarily dazzled. She was wearing a strapless blue evening dress without a scrap of jewellery, and the familiar room suddenly seemed strange—a dimension of myself I was noticing for the first time now as she was discreetly taking stock of it. I had never thought of it as sordid before. The hideous carpet had been stained into neutrality by ink and whiskey. Time and tobacco had mellowed the stucco wallpaper. And the two armchairs, once expressive of Mrs. Roddie's ideas about luxury, had now been sat into the mould of my own aggressive laziness.

"Your landlady?" Josephine enquired. "How do you manage to put up with her?" She wanted to say 'how can you live in such a room?'

"I can put up with anybody who puts up with me. Actually

she dotes on me because I resemble her favourite nephew, who died of infantile paralysis. Mrs. Roddie stands between me and the world, so that I can work, when I absolutely have to, in perfect peace and isolation. She also waits on me hand and foot: which for a man like me, without any family, is the greatest luxury in the world."

"Wouldn't it be more comfortable to get married?" Her eyes rested on a photograph of my mother, large-bosomed and challenging.

"Not for the sake of getting married, no. Some of my friends accuse me of masochism, others of affectation. But when I consider their marriages—premature, hasty and complicated—I can't help thinking that they might have been saved if they had been settled comfortably in digs with a guardian dragon to keep the girls off. I can never understand why more bachelors of my sort of standing don't take advantage of the inexpensive bliss offered them by lonely women like Mrs. Roddie."

"But she doesn't seem to succeed in keeping off the women. After all, here I am, and for all she knows I might be threatening your very existence as a bachelor!"

"I can afford to take a risk now and then. Actually, she's more frightened of losing me than I am of being thrown out. Though she threatens me about once a week, she's a conservative old man-o'-war—she has more talent for repelling boarders than she has for sailing after new prizes."

I settled down with a whiskey and soda, and Josephine, after some persuasion, allowed me to adulterate her soda-water.

I said nervously: "Now let's get down to business. What about Somerset House?"

"No luck there. There are two Millington-Forsetts in the last five years, brothers of the one we're after."

31

"And what about the *Peerage and Baronetage?*"

She searched in a white silk bag sown with pearls and produced a slip of paper. " 'Claude Nevil Millington-Forsett, third son of the fourth baronet. Born 1859.' The editor hasn't been in touch with him since 1928 and then only indirectly through a sister who is called Mrs. Danby and lives in Fulham —No. 12, Gladstone Road."

I already knew about Mrs. Danby and I had merely wanted to test Josephine. "How did you manage to get all this so quickly?" I asked. "I thought you were working this afternoon."

"I was. But Mr. Hodge was down at the printer's. I got my mother to do Somerset House. The rest I did by telephone."

"Do you mean to say that the *Peerage* gave you all that over the phone?"

"Well, not exactly. They told me they had made enquiries themselves in 1928, but that the family of the gentleman in question had absolutely no information about him. The man I spoke to obviously didn't realize who Claude Nevil is, or was—he merely sympathized with me as a fellow genealogist barking up the wrong family-tree!"

"How did you find out about Mrs. Danby?"

"She was in the *Baronetage* too, of course, and since she was the only one apart from Claude Nevil not listed as being dead—she's ten years younger than him, actually—I looked her up in the telephone book, and there, by a stroke of luck, she was."

"But there are dozens of Danbys in the telephone book, aren't there? Are you sure she's the right one?"

"Certain. I rang her up as the secretary of Mr. Budge, the man I spoke to at the *Peerage and Baronetage*, and asked her if she had anything to add for our next edition. I was just going to ask her if she had any information about Claude

Nevil when, quite honestly, I lost my nerve. There was something about her voice that scared me. She sounded old, angry and a bit mad, and I thought perhaps you would do it better than me. . . ."

I said: "You've done a wonderful job and you were quite right to stop where you did. Mrs. Danby will need very careful handling—it's just possible she does know about her brother, but won't give anything away."

Josephine gave me one of those swift personal looks that I was beginning to find intensely agreeable. "You'll let me know at once, won't you? I shall be on tenterhooks until I hear. When I think of *us* being even remotely involved in a historic murder-case, everything else seems dull by comparison. It's like living in fiction, isn't it?"

After this flight her eyes abruptly stopped shining. She looked at her watch and said "My dear, you're *ruined*! It's half-past twelve."

As we walked up the street towards the taxi-rank at Victoria there was a slight fog coming up from the river and the streetlamps had a debauched look.

"Ugh!" she shivered and took my arm. "How can you bear to live in this sinister locality?"

As we parted she flattered my ego in a different way— "You can tell Mrs. Hudson, if she doesn't know it already, that I only stayed three-quarters of an hour."

"Mrs. Roddie," I corrected her. "This isn't Baker Street, you know!"

"Did I really say Hudson?" She laughed. "Well, if you will get silly girls to help you you must expect to be put on a pedestal!"

I slept badly that night, between exciting thoughts about Josephine and the disagreeable prospect of interviewing Mrs.

Danby. Far from cancelling out, the two themes fed each other. When I gave Josephine the job of looking up the *Peerage and Baronetage*, I had known that Mrs. Danby was the logical end of the enquiry. Had I also hoped unconsciously that she would do the dirty work for me? Or had I hoped for just what had happened, to be egged on by feminine weakness to take a step I hadn't dared to take alone? In the silence of the night, broken by occasional footsteps and the regular sorties of the cuckoo from Mrs. Roddie's clock on the landing, I thought myself unworthy of the romantic notions I was beginning to inspire in Josephine, and I decided that the only way to keep up the pretence was to find some moral courage—and quickly. The truth was that I was as lightly boiled as any of the poets Josephine seemed to cultivate in between society beaux. It was one thing to write with spirit about Millington-Forsett and revel in the Conan Doyle atmosphere. Another to meet Mrs. Danby, *née* Millington-Forsett, and face the reality behind the literary genre, the private effects of public events. What had I cared, when writing my essay, about the possible existence of an old lady who had the misfortune to be the sister of the murderer? If I succeeded in meeting her in the flesh, would I have the nerve to argue, with my journalist friends, that the duty of informing the public overrides all respect for private feeling?

I woke dream-tossed and aggressive, and was confirmed in my mood by the absence of bacon with my eggs.

"Your having told me about it doesn't make any difference," I snapped at Mrs. Roddie. "You shouldn't have bought salt bacon—that's all there is to it."

"What's eating you, Mr. Kennington?" she asked with sadistic mildness. "Maybe it's that feemul you were *entertaining* last night?"

"She was *not* a 'female'—that's to say, she was a beautiful, charming and intelligent girl. And if you want to know what's eating me the answer is sodium chloride."

After a wash and a shave and a glance at the paper, I dressed and went down to the telephone.

The ringing tone went on so long that I began to hope she was out. Then there was a crackle and a voice said "Well?"

"Hullo," I said, "is that Mrs. Danby? This is Mr. Kennington."

"Ah, Mr. Pennington, what news of my poor Emily?"

"Mr. *Kennington*—Raymond Kennington, the author."

"I've never heard of you and I don't like authors. What do you want?"

"I should like news of your brother."

Silence. Mewing in the background. Then: "My brothers are all dead."

My heart began to beat faster: "Surely not Mr. Claude Nevil Millington-Forsett?"

"As far as I'm concerned he's been dead for years. And if you wish to rake up the past, I would advise you to wait until I am dead too. I have suffered too much from people like you, and I only wish to be left alone."

"Perhaps, if you can spare half an hour some time, you will allow me to come and talk to you?"

"You are talking to me now. What more do you want?"

"But the telephone is so impersonal. I feel that if I could meet you personally you would not deny me the help I so badly need."

"What's the matter? Is Nevil . . .? No, I absolutely refuse. It would be different if you had anything to tell me about him."

I thought quickly. She was about to slam the door in my face and I had to get a foot in it. Merely to meet her would

35

be an extraordinary experience—the only opportunity I might ever have of getting first-hand information about the elusive hero of my essay. The idea came to me just in time.

"As a matter of fact I *have* something to tell you, or I shall have in a few days. May I come and see you then?"

"You may telephone again and I'll consider it. I don't want strangers in my flat unless I know a great deal more about them than I know about you. You say you are an author. What is your name again?"

"Raymond Kennington."

"And the name of your publisher?"

"Hodge and Ricketts."

"Very well then. Goodbye, Mr. Kennington."

CHAPTER THREE

Yours Truly, Alfred J. Moxon

IT WAS THREE DAYS before I reported to Josephine. I had
been asked by a Crime Club in Balliol to read a paper on
the Background of the Murderer, and being in awe of Oxford
in general and of Balliol in particular, like a fool I took it
seriously. I expected, that is, to be taken seriously. I saw
earnest young intellectuals sitting at my feet, and in my
anxiety not to reveal what those feet were made of, I let
myself in for far more work than I had foreseen when I accepted the invitation. When I tried to think constructively
about the background of the murderer I realized that, for all
my pretences in print, it was still a complete mystery to me.
To get something that sounded authoritative I had to consult
the secretary of the Howard League and pass a long dry
evening with a remote female relative who was a magistrate
in the Juvenile Courts.

All the time I was working on my paper, Millington-Forsett was in my mind. I had been pleased with my title, *A Twist
Somewhere*. But as I ploughed into psychology and statistics,
reports of Probation Officers and Prison Governers, it became increasingly clear to me that the type of criminal I
depended on for my daily bread was almost obsolete by contemporary standards. My essays cashed in on the villainous-
ness of villains, not on the obscure tangle of influences that
explained away criminality: one could not write essays about
sexual perverts, or if one did, nobody was likely to read
them. The more I read about Lobotomy and Broken Homes,
the more I appreciated Millington-Forsett. His crime (crimes?)
might have been committed specially for me to write about.
Nobody, in all the newspaper publicity attendant on his trial,

had suggested that there was anything wrong with his father and mother: nobody had been able to extract anything relevant from his old nurse, or discover any abnormality about his adolescence as a fag at Eton. And whatever Mrs. Danby might be persuaded to say about him I felt confident that it wouldn't diminish his stature.

In writing about the background of the murderer I tried so hard not to be superficial (reviewers had sometimes accused me of this) that I managed to produce a script totally unlike myself or my writing. I was dined in an oak-panelled room in Balliol, and so well wined by amusing and lively undergraduates, that by the time I came to read my paper I was ready to flop in every sense. And, in fact, though they were charming and hospitable, it was clear from the conversation that succeeded the reading that most of them had been bored to tears. They were not interested in Lombroso, Tuke or Freud. They had wanted, not a series of case-histories, with statistics and quotations from authorities, but a sparkling recital of my own personal adventures in the murk of London's underworld. I was forced to admit, with an honesty that seemed almost churlish, that the nearest I had ever got to a murderer, apart from hobnobbing with the waxworks in the Chamber of Horrors, was the public gallery at the Old Bailey. But I saved myself from utter disgrace by hinting that I was at present engaged in an exciting investigation they might like to hear about one day. Like Josephine, they had been misled by the blurb on the back of my books into thinking of me as a romantic figure, and I realized for the second time that writers on crime are not as other authors. They are expected to have blood on their fingers.

I returned from the experience with a thick head and a fiercer determination to hunt down my quarry.

"Mr. Hodge"—Josephine told me—"is tearing his hair,

or would be if he had any. He was appalled when he heard that you had gone to Oxford to read a paper to undergraduates. He thinks you don't realize how urgent it is to clear up the Millington-Forsett mystery."

"God!" I exploded, "it's only four days since I saw him, and look at the ground I've already covered. Does he imagine that Millington-Forsett puts his name and address in the telephone book?"

"Ssh!" said Josephine, casting a furtive glance round the almost empty cocktail bar, "there are two men sitting just behind us waggling cauliflower ears. Hasn't it occurred to you that the pursuit of our friend may involve risk?"

"Oh come, Josephine. It's exciting enough without trying to frighten ourselves. If the old man could hear you he would be flattered to know that the new generation still regards him with superstition."

"All the same," she said, "it isn't exactly comfortable. He may still be capable of biting . . . Well, don't torture me any longer. Did you manage to have a talk with his sister?"

I described my conversation with Mrs. Danby, adding—it had struck me since—"if he's alive, I think she would like to see him again. He may have treated her very badly, but blood being thicker than mud, it wouldn't surprise me if she still thought of him as her older brother, the last survivor of her family. Anyway, I've got a little more to go on now. Have a look at these two letters."

Directly after my talk with Mrs. Danby I had put an advertisement in *The Times* requesting anybody who had information about the whereabouts or recent activities of Claude Nevil Millington-Forsett to get in touch with a box-number. On my return from Oxford I had gone straight from Paddington to Printing House Square, where the letters were waiting for me. The first, posted in Hammersmith, was written

39

on a bit of paper roughly torn off a notepad. It was written in a flowery uneducated hand, and bore no address, date or signature.

Sir,

I write these lines to tell you not to put your nose in others bisness if you dont want to get it birnt.

Josephine shrugged her shoulders. "Might be anybody. An old servant of the family? A 'bisness' acquaintance?"

"Or just some hooligan. There are people who get quite a kick out of writing mysterious anonymous letters. Anyway, it doesn't get us any further. It merely suggests the obscure world in which Millington-Forsett lives. But look at the other letter. That's much more interesting."

It bore a Brixton postmark and the address was 16 Crick Road, S.W.2.

Dear Sir,

In response to your appeal for information about Mr. Claude Nevil Millington-Forsett, I believe I may be in a position to help you. If you will acquaint me with the reason for your enquiry, I shall be glad to communicate what I know.

Yours truly,
Alfred J. Moxon

Josephine whistled softly: "This sounds promising, doesn't it? If only he didn't live in Brixton, it would be very promising indeed. Even darkest Pimlico would be more healthy . . ."

"And if he didn't want to know the reason for my enquiry. That strikes me as nosey, if not actually fishy."

"But your advertisement may have sounded nosey to him, if not actually fishy. After all, you might be the police, or a rival creditor of Claude Nevil's. If you have to be guarded, so has he . . . I say, *you don't think?*'—Josephine looked at me with a wild surmise, then drained her Martini at one gulp—*"you don't think it could be Claude Nevil himself?"*

"Admirable, my dear Watson," I said, "but you have omitted to compare Moxon's writing with the facsimile of the document drawn up by Millington-Forsett, signed by the unfortunate Sir George Richmond and reproduced in the Lamont book. No, Claude Nevil—unless he has changed his hand completely—couldn't possibly have written this letter. And it would surprise me if he has come down as low as Brixton after pocketing those enormous damages only ten years ago. But let's try and find out what sort of a chap the writer is. First the notepaper—good quality, but slightly yellowed with age—he's poor, but knows what's what and wants to make a good impression—he keeps this notepaper for state occasions. Grammar, style and spelling are educated. But it's pompous, isn't it?—though not quite the contemporary stilted style: that's his natural way of writing to strangers and to me it suggests an old man. I think the pen also points to that—it looks as if he uses a J nib. And notice the S in 'position'—he's brought the tail of it down to the next line to fill in the gap between 'the' and 'reason'; he probably paused before writing 'reason', possibly rejecting a cruder phrase—anyway he fills in the gap because he belongs to a generation that liked manuscripts to look nice. His writing is good, but the loops have gone a bit angular and his hand has trembled on the upstroke of the Q in 'acquainted' —that also points to advanced age. As for the general picture —writing and style in relation to address and notepaper—they give the impression of an old man fallen on evil days . . . and one who has richly deserved it."

Josephine said: "Amazing! But I don't quite follow the last bit—why has he richly deserved to fall on evil days?"

"Oh, that's pure guesswork. A respectable man of good antecedents doesn't go and live in Brixton unless he has been rejected by his own class."

Josephine rubbed her hands with glee. "Better and better. And now you have shown me your methods, even I can't help noticing something. The signature is more carefully written than the rest of the letter, as if Alfred J. Moxon were a name he doesn't write normally—do you agree?"

"That's brilliant," I said. "I believe you're right."

"You do? Well, I don't! I think it would be safer to assume that his normal signature is illegible, and that's why he wrote his name so carefully. What do you think of that, Holmes?"

"I think it's very clever and very beastly, and I give you warning now that I'm not used to being teased, especially by women. Come on, let's have another drink—we've got to work out a reply."

Excited by a second cocktail Josephine was all for going to Brixton herself to check up on Alfred J. Moxon. She couldn't rid herself of the morbid notion that he was either Claude Nevil or some crony of his, and that a hideous web was being spun for me in the shadow of the walls of Brixton Prison. "Let's keep a sense of proportion," I protested, "Claude Nevil, if alive, will be eighty next year. And so long as my book isn't published he can't do a thing to me. Suppose we give up trying to be too clever and write a straightforward letter explaining the facts?"

Dear Sir [I wrote],

In reply to the question in your letter, the reason for enquiry is that I am preparing a book about the murder-trial in which Mr. Millington-Forsett once figured. As I am advised that it is dangerous to publish anything about the case until I have definite evidence that he is dead, I would welcome any information which will enable me to trace him since 1928, the year of his last public appearance.

Yours truly,

Raymond Kennington

Josephine did not conceal her opinion that this approach was unsubtle and amateurish. She wanted me to pretend that I was the London Library trying to recover some lost books, a Sunday newspaper offering money for the Millington-Forsett life-story, or a family solicitor with something of interest to communicate—anything in fact but what I really was. My pride had been slightly hurt by her laughing at my brilliant deductions, and I was rather more scornful than I need have been about her suggestions for approaching Moxon. She left rather abruptly to keep a dinner engagement with somebody called Gerald Harbury, who was all the more obviously a lord because she carefully avoided mentioning the title.

Left alone, when I had hoped to have dinner with her myself, I came to the conclusion that I was more likely to get on with both Millington-Forsett and Josephine if I didn't mix the two together. Josephine, I decided, as I vented my spleen on Mrs. Roddie's steak, was not interested in me for myself.

Two days later I had a reply from Moxon.

Dear Mr. Kennington,

I last saw Mr. Millington-Forsett in the autumn of 1932. He was then staying in this house under the style of Mr. Percy Shelley.

As he seemed very much down on his luck and emaciated by a stomach cancer I felt sorry for him and lent him some of my meagre savings to enable him to try a new treatment.

Imagine my disgust and chagrin when he suddenly did a

bunk, after paying the landlady, but not me. It was only then that I discovered his true identity. The landlady, who is a most respectable woman, was horrified to find under his bed a newspaper clipping containing a photograph of him taken outside the law courts in 1928. Despite the removal of the small beard he then affected, there could be no doubt that Mr. Percy Shelley was none other than Claude Nevil Millington-Forsett! What hurt me and my landlady—she too had felt sorry for him and given him special terms—was that he must have had plenty of money all the time.

So you see, my dear Sir, I am as interested in finding him alive as you are in finding him dead. But my opinion is that he is most unlikely to be still with us. He was a very sick man six years ago and even if he were still alive he would hardly be in a position to embark on a libel action. If I were you I would not hesitate to proceed with the publication of the book.

In conclusion, may I wish you success, and express the hope that in return for the small service I have been able to render you, you will have the kindness to send me a copy of the work. Since discovering the real identity of Mr. Percy Shelley I have myself become interested in his chequered past and would be extremely glad to learn more.

Yours sincerely,

Alfred J. Moxon

This letter so excited me that I hurried round to Hodge and gave a full report of my investigations up to date. I ended enthusiastically: "What with Patterson's story and Moxon's letter, and what I hope to get out of his sister, it looks as if the second edition of *A Twist Somewhere* is going to be wagged by its tail."

"All in good time," said Hodge drily. "Let's not start counting our chickens. I agree you've found out a lot. But what in fact does it all add up to? Millington-Forsett was alive six years ago and still in good money-making form. Though stomach cancer is, I believe, usually fatal, I have heard of cases where surgery has prolonged life for several years. Don't you think you could get more out of Moxon by paying him a little visit in Brixton? He sounds forthcoming—almost too forthcoming. Let me see . . . what was it that struck me as odd?" He put on his spectacles, and Josephine, who had been bustling in and out of the room with a look of complete disinterest, suddenly sat down at a desk in the corner and started furiously flipping through a card-index, casting cold glances in my direction. Obviously I had done something wrong.

"Ah yes," Hodge was saying, "there's one phrase in this letter that strikes me as completely incongruous. I wonder if you noticed it too?"

"You mean where he says Millington-Forsett 'did a bunk'? —too slangy for Alfred J. Moxon?"

"Exactly."

"And coming after 'imagine my disgust and chagrin' it almost suggests that he thinks the whole thing a hell of a joke?"

"Exactly. I thought your trained mind wouldn't miss that."

"Well, what of it?"

"I just wondered, that's all. . . . I mean, he doesn't sound exactly reliable, does he? You agree with me that we shouldn't go ahead without probing a bit deeper? After all, he might be provoking you to publish!"

Curiously enough, that hadn't struck me, and I could see Josephine's eyes flashing ironically, like a lighthouse to a ship already on the rocks.

"Of course I agree. I just wanted you to know that I

haven't been idle. Personally I would be prepared to take the risk. But I certainly don't expect you to. As a matter of fact I'm lunching with a friend from Scotland Yard. If that's negative—and those people are about as communicative as insulating tape—I'll go down to Brixton this afternoon."

At the very mention of Scotland Yard Hodge looked at me with more respect.

"Well, I'm very glad to hear you haven't been letting the grass grow under your feet. I hope you don't think I've been trying to teach you your job? By the way, if there's any purely routine stuff, Miss Canning might be prepared to give you a hand, mightn't you, Miss Canning?"

"Yes, yes," said Josephine heartily, then murmured something inaudible.

"For instance," pursued Hodge, "if you want to try Somerset House again and look him up under the name of Shelley, I could spare her for an hour or so this afternoon . . . you don't think that would be much use? Well, you never know. We can't afford not to be thorough and I know your time is valuable."

I went, leaving my hat on the chair, in the hope that Josephine would take the hint. She did. She caught me lingering on the doorstep and thrust my hat into my hand.

"So you're not telling me any more?" she said. "You and Hodge can arrange the whole thing better without the interference of any tiresome female?"

"But, Josephine," I stammered, "what's the matter?" It was the first time I had ever seen her look fierce, and my dismay was mixed with admiraiton.

"You went straight to Mr. Hodge with that exciting letter without showing it to me first; you never breathed a word to me about Scotland Yard. I'm only good for Somerset House!"

"As a matter of fact I rang you twice, once at your home and once at the office. But it's difficult to collaborate effectively with somebody who has such an important social life. You know better than I do how worried Hodge is. By the way, what was the matter with him today? I thought his tone rather unpleasant."

"I do wish you wouldn't call him 'Hodge' in that contemptuous way."

"Well, I've heard you call him Hodge yourself, but let that pass; what was the matter with him?"

"Oh, it's that Modern Poetry Series. Didn't you see the reviews of Gregory Drooley's slim volume? Rather sickening after Alec's recommendation and that stirring preface by Sean O'Seolinn. One was headed IRISH STEW WITHOUT MEAT. He'd been looking through them before you came in, and what really put him in a bad temper was when Ricketts said 'I told you so!' Ricketts was against the whole project from the beginning, but he has a vague feeling of inferiority about poetry and I've heard him admit rather grudgingly that a bit of poetry, now and then, makes a publisher's list more respectable."

"I see. And when Hodge saw me, he immediately associated me with Ricketts? He's never quite got over the shame of having a crime-writer on his list."

"Oh, rubbish. He knows which side his bread's buttered. Anyway, I must go back now or Mr. Hodge will begin to think the worst—he has moments of behaving like your landlady."

For the second time I had the uncomfortable feeling that she had been talking for the sake of talking. Something was happening to me, or to her, or to both of us: too little had been said, and too much. Things might go either way, and clearly one of us was intended by nature to weaken.

She said goodbye, smiling rather stiffly, then turned and walked quickly away. Then, while I was still standing watching her, she turned again and came back. "Raymond," she said, and I realized with a shock that it was the first time she had used my Christian name. "*Please* take me with you to Brixton—I just can't bear not to be in on this *now* ... now please don't say no—I'll pose as your wife, your daughter or your grandmother—any relative you like—and if you want proof that I can do it, ring up Mervyn Sellars. He once offered me a stage part as a pretty housemaid because he said I had a naturally 'supporting' face!"

I looked hard at that supporting face and decided that it was too eloquent for the part she wanted or thought she wanted.

"No," I said brutally—"you can't come. We don't know each other well enough to be sure we won't pull in different directions. This is reality. A lot of money depends on it—it isn't just a romantic game. But if you can bear to come and dine at my digs tonight, Mrs. Roddie has laid on a pheasant which has come all the way from her brother in Renfrew and is simply clamouring to melt in somebody's mouth."

"Thank you," she said without hesitation. "I don't want to butt in on Mrs. Roddie's brother's pheasant, and anyway my stepfather has invited me to eat larks' tongues with him at the Drapers' Dinner."

Behind my lunch with Bairstow at the Criterion, there was quite a history. Shorthand is about the only accomplishment I have ever learnt. Conscious of being superior in this respect to most males, I have sedulously kept it up. Years ago I formed the habit of recording conversations in buses and trains in the belief that one day it would pay dividends. Even now, when I climb on a public transport I look for a seat behind couples who are talking, avoiding newspaper-readers like the plague. Incidentally, this may be the reason why I have never been good at artistic dialogues. When I try and write fiction the characters become as flat as their real-life models whose conversation I try and reproduce from notes. But if I hadn't known shorthand I should never have known Bairstow and I should have known less about Millington-Forsett.

In a bus between Oxford Circus and Euston I recorded a conversation which was so like the dialogue in a gangster film that I got out sooner than I had intended to, just to look at the two men behind me and note the details of their appearance. Two days later, glancing through my paper at breakfast, I read about a burglary in Kensington. Certain names and descriptions seemed vaguely reminiscent and looking up the notes I had recorded on the bus I became convinced that the men I had overheard had been discussing this very crime. I took my shorthand notes to Scotland Yard and described the men. Within twenty-four hours both were arrested, and as a result of this extraordinary coincidence the C.I.D. rounded up a whole gang that had been troubling them for months.

Bairstow was the detective in charge of the case. He was grateful for the good turn I had done him and when he discovered that I was the author of *Black Museum* he became extremely friendly with me. But from the beginning it was an artificial relationship, a friendship of interests rather than temperaments, and as soon as I had learnt something about police methods and he had touched the bottom of my knowledge of the history of crime, we agreed tacitly to let it lapse. He was, I believe, a first-rate detective. He had worked his way right up the ladder by sheer efficiency and hard grind. But his personality did not seem to have developed in proportion. His breezy approach, when he greeted you, gave way all too soon to the basic woodenness of the constable, and he had a maddening habit of whistling through his teeth and tapping on the table as though he could hardly wait till you had stopped talking.

He was doing this all the time I was telling him the tale of my trouble over Millington-Forsett, and the whistling and the tapping only made me prolix. When I had finished he sat back in his chair and rubbed his finger-tips together.

"Well, old man," he said heartily, "I know you once helped us out of a hole and, believe you me, I'm grateful to you. But look at it from the Yard's point of view. You were only doing your duty as a member of the public. But unfortunately, much as I would like personally to help you, it's not my duty as an officer of the law—in fact it's not in the public interest. This isn't a detective story in which the police carry on like race-course tipsters."

He was enjoying being powerful and mysterious. He gave the impression that he knew a great deal about Millington-Forsett, and I was not going to be fobbed off with his official manner.

"Look here," I said, "come and dine with me tonight at Strang's, and if you can hold out against the meal I shall give you, I shall begin to think you're a real policeman!"

He didn't want to be unfriendly. He accepted, only to ring up in the afternoon with a transparent excuse. He must have thought it over and decided that I was trying to bribe him. I went to see him again next day.

"Bairstow," I said, "I deserve better of you. I just want you to try and be as human as I know you can be. After all, I'm not asking you to give away any official secrets—if so, you would surely have told me so without beating about the bush. At the very least you owe me an explanation of why you should protect criminals like Millington-Forsett from discreet enquirers like myself, but not vice versa. If that's democracy, I'm for Hitler!"

My appeal seemed to touch him—whether humanly or politically I couldn't discover. He agreed to have lunch with me. But I remember that lunch, coming, as it did, directly after my interview with Hodge and my tiff with Josephine, as one of the most frustrating experiences of my life. He spent the first half-hour telling me that he couldn't possibly divulge any information—'in my position'—'you don't seem to realize'—'if everybody did the same as you' etc. When I suggested that he was talking for the files, he flushed angrily and said that England wasn't Germany. I pegged away at him, while he drummed on the table and whistled through his teeth, till finally, when I had threatened to go over his head, he sighed deeply and said: "Well, the fact is *we don't know!*"

"*You don't know?*" I was fiercely incredulous. He had found sand in the oysters. He had recognized the waiter as one of his 'protégés' (which probably accounted for the sand). And he had put away half a bottle of excellent claret without finding anything better to say than 'not bad' (smack, smack), 'but a bit sour to my way of thinking'. But I still couldn't believe he had deliberately led me up the garden path.

"No, I'm afraid not," he said, momentarily humbled. "The fact is, we kept tapes on him till 1930, when he was reported to be living in style in Dublin under the alias of Captain Davenport, running a Career Bureau for Girls. Our information was that this was only a cover, that all the time he was head of a racket which procured Irish and English girls for continental brothels with false promises of domestic employment. But when the Dublin police closed in on his office they got nothing out of the raid but a bunch of punks who could hardly speak a word of English. After that we just stopped bothering about him."

I felt bitter: "So you just stopped bothering about him, did you? It may interest you to know that in 1932 he was still alive and swindling."

"Oh really?" Bairstow could hardly afford to seem interested. "Well, whatever the source of your information, we reckon he must be harmless by now. And if the Yard has given up worrying you can bet your boots he's either behaving himself or dead. . . ."

I looked at my watch: "Good Lord, I must be going—I have a date with my 'source' in Brixton. If I drag up Millington-Forsett's corpse, I'll send you a copy of the death-certificate—so that you can bring your files up to date!"

That penetrated Bairstow's hide. "Thanks, friend," he said. "I'm sure Records will be much indebted to you. But as an old hand at systematic dragging for corpses my advice to amateurs is 'Keep off the mud!' We don't want to have to file *your* death-certificate!"

'Pompous ass!' I thought, and went my way fuming at officialdom, though not altogether displeased with myself.

CHAPTER FOUR

'There was an old war-horse called Shelley'

MY LONDON was more comprehensive than Josephine's. It included Hammersmith and Fulham, and even at a pinch my birthplace. Though I had migrated from Stoke Newington to Pimlico immediately after my mother's death and never set foot in the place since, the drearier areas of London were still part of my visual landscape. Whereas for Josephine, whose London consisted of the West End, including Chelsea, Kensington and Regent's Park, all that lay beyond was socially and aesthetically beyond the pale. Nothing existed—not even the classier suburbs—until one reached the really bucolic country.

Yet about Brixton we were agreed. Apart from its association with the Prison (Wandsworth and Holloway were unthinkable for the same reason) the name evoked a picture of mean brick houses in serried rows, a sordid hinterland bereft of character or *raison d'être* but the disastrous fertility of the Victorian poor.

It was foggy as I left Victoria, but by the time the conductor set me down in the Brixton Road, the fog had thinned and whitened sufficiently to enable me to read the names of the streets. Crick Street was quite a step, and as I drew away from the traffic of the main road, I was assailed by the silence and the gloom, as well as by a persistent smell of gas. At the same time I had a pleasing sense of my own adventurousness in penetrating alone into hostile territory: the Millington-Forsett legend had become so real to me that a district no drabber than nine-tenths of London suggested superior evil at every turn. Stumbling unexpectedly on an L.C.C. sign which said CRICK STREET S.W.2 my heart beat so fast that I had to stop and light a cigarette before I could proceed in search of No. 16.

Crick Street was rather less grim than most. The street was wider and the houses bigger, standing back from small ill-kempt gardens. No. 16 had a hedge of sparse laurel and a flower-bed decked with the winter skeletons of hydrangeas. Its brass door-knocker had recently been cleaned and through the lace curtains of a first-floor window shone a light that looked benign by Brixton standards.

Waiting on the doorsteps of strange houses I always try to forget my nervousness by trying to picture the person who will open to me. Mr. Moxon had spoken of his landlady as 'a very respectable woman', which led me to expect a Mrs. Roddie. I was not at all prepared for the fortyish person who eventually responded to my timid knocking. Her lips were red and approximate, her hair (peroxide) was in curlers, and she was enveloped—very carelessly considering her figure—in a peacock-coloured dressing-gown. The only ostensibly respectable thing about her was the gold cross that hung round her neck. I put her down as the landlady's daughter, dolling up for a tea-dance at the local palais.

"You must excuse me," I said, "I seem to have come at an awkward time. Is Mr. Moxon in?"

She had switched on the porch light and now she peered at me for a moment without answering. "Well, he isn't," she said in a peaty brogue; "is it business you've come to see him about?"

"I'm afraid I can't explain. But my name is Kennington. Mr. Moxon would know what I've come about."

I detected an easing of the tension, confirmed by the care with which she repeated my name. "Kennington, like the

Oval, is it? Well, if I might trouble you to come back in half an hour Mr. Moxon will be in for his tea."

I took her word that he was out and walked about Brixton in the gathering gloom, chain-smoking and consulting my watch under the street lamps. Exactly half an hour later I was admitted to No. 16 and shown upstairs—to the room that had been lit all the time.

A lanky old man rose from the low box-like armchair in which he had been crouching over the fire. He had deep-set eyes shaded by unkempt bushy eyebrows that looked black in contrast with his white hair.

"My dear Sir, I'm delighted to see you, though I had hardly hoped you would spare the time to call on an obscure correspondent. I must tell you, I am something of a recluse. I have had much bitterness in my life, but here, away from the worse associations of better days, I have found peace at last among simple, unpretentious people."

"Your landlady certainly seems homely," I groped. Even more disconcerting than the cavernousness of Moxon's eye-sockets, which made it very difficult to judge his expression, was a sporadic tic of the right eyelid: he seemed to be winking at me—as one rogue to another.

"Mrs. Kernan? Oh yes, she *is* homely. A free and easy Irish girl who puts up with my little foibles and ministers to my simple needs. She too has known what it is to suffer: that is why she is so tolerant. Really I have been more fortunate than I deserve." He paused for a moment and brooded over the gas-fire. Then abruptly: "But my dear Sir, you are still standing . . . well now, have you something to tell me about our mutual friend Mr. Percy Shelley?"

"I'm afraid not. I was rather hoping to persuade you to tell me a bit more about him. If I had a better picture of the man and his habits I might stumble on something which would enable me to pick up his traces; perhaps in the end to recover your money. I suppose you have an IOU?"

Moxon gave a dry cackle which did not agree with his way of speaking. "My dear Sir, I wasn't born yesterday, though Mrs. Kernan sometimes tells me I am entering my second childhood!" Then, as though ashamed of this undignified outburst: "What about a little stimulant? This wretched fire barely keeps the cold at bay, let alone the gloom of the London winter."

While he was fumbling in a cupboard, I took a look round the room. Basically it was enough to drive a man to drink. The floor was covered with steel-blue linoleum, and the furniture, a mass-produced dining-room suite, was made of pine stained the colour of nicotine. But it was relieved by personal touches: there were some hunting prints on the walls and the bookcase was filled with autumnal stains of cheap thrillers, interspersed with sere accumulations of old Tauchnitz.

"You are interested in my books?" he said, setting down two large brandies and a siphon. "I have aroused your professional curiosity?"

"Professional?" Did he take me for a detective?

"Well, you say you are an author, and I have every reason to believe you. In fact I took a stroll to the Library yesterday and borrowed what promises to be a very entertaining volume. I have it here on the top of the cupboard. Well, here's to your health, Sir, and to the success of your forthcoming book! By the way, I never asked you if you shared my taste for brandy and soda? A comforting Victorian drink. I have flirted with many drinks, and loved wine: but brandy and soda is the only drink I have ever espoused!"

I sipped. He took a gulp which emptied a third of his glass, sucking his lips over his dentures with a curious, senile sensuality. "That's better. I feel more fluent immediately. Nowadays I see so few people of my own class that I find my tongue getting stiffer and stiffer. For me this is a real privilege."

I murmured politely, and he went on, relaxed: "I will gladly tell you all I know about Mr. Shelley, but before I begin, what makes you think he is still alive? I told you that when I last saw him six years ago, he was a stricken man?"

"But perhaps he wasn't as ill as he seemed. After all, he did do a bunk. Mr. Shelley was an old soldier and old soldiers never die!"

Again the dry cackle. This time I accepted it as a compliment.

"My dear Mr. Kennington, the man was already a skeleton. He spent most of the day in bed, and in pain, which he had to alleviate by constant drug-taking. He was visibly a dying man."

"But isn't it just possible he deceived you about the nature of his illness?"

Moxon shook his head solemnly: "It is just possible that he might have deceived *me*, but he could hardly have deceived Mrs. Kernan, who happens to be a trained nurse. He had already been operated upon and the surgeons advised against a second operation. His only hope was to find a new treatment, and though I could not share his faith in homeopathy, I could not refuse him his only hope."

"All right then. You lent him money for some homeopathic treatment. Surely we can find out who he went to? Failing that we could try the London hospitals, we could . . ."

"You are young and optimistic, Mr. Kennington. We have no guarantee that the name I knew him under was the name he used in other parts of London, and as far as homeopaths are concerned I wouldn't put any money on your chances. But unless you are prepared to spend months on research, you will be wise to begin at Somerset House."

It was my turn to say 'I wasn't born yesterday', but I contented myself with a knowing smile and shifted my attack to another quarter.

"Could you let me see the newspaper cutting he left behind? It struck me that you and your landlady might have been mistaken about his identity. If he was so emaciated, his appearance must have changed considerably."

Moxon got up and poured me another drink. Then he went to the cupboard and returned with a small attaché case made of false leather. He had a bundle of newspaper cuttings clipped together and he fumbled for some moments before he found the one he wanted.

"There you are," he said, and while I was studying the photograph, which was set in a yellowed *Evening Star* report, he went to the door and called: "Mrs. Kernan, will you come up a moment, please?"

Mrs. Kernan appeared, treading rather delicately, I thought; but that may have been due to the height of her heels, for she was obviously dressed up to be killed.

"Mrs. Kernan, this gentleman is a friend of mine who is interested in the fate of Mr. Percy Shelley. Now, what makes you so sure that this photograph you found under his bed is really of him? Mightn't it be just a strong resemblance?"

"No, it mightn't. It's himself all right and no mistake about it. Sure, how could I make a mistake when I had him three weeks in this house, taking up meals every day because I was sorry for him not being able to go round the corner to Polatti's —and anyway, why would he be keeping the clipping if it wasn't of himself in his palmy days?"

"Yes, yes, but wasn't there anything else that happened to confirm your opinion that he was Millington-Forsett?"

"Well there was"—she shut the door and drew up a chair— "and if you'll give me a drink I'll tell this gentleman about it. . . . Thank you, just a nip, and I'll take it straight . . . well now, it was the night before the gentleman left. He said he was feeling a bit rum—it was always 'rum' when he felt queer—and would I go to the pub and buy him a drop of brandy to help him with the pain in his stomach? 'Now, Colonel,' I said—I used to call him 'Colonel' because he was forever telling me about the wars he had fought in—'Colonel, I won't do it. You'll be after dying on me instead of getting well.' 'Go on,' he says, 'or you may suffer the same torments in hell.' Well, I know I shouldn't have, but I did it. I bought him a whole half-bottle. 'Now go easy,' I said, 'and mind, I won't hear any more of your blasphemies!'

"Well, at ten o'clock I heard him come out of the bath-room to fill his hot-water bottle. He was laughing and talking away to himself and at first I thought he had company—you'd be surprised the visitors he had, an old man like that complaining of loneliness and sickness. Anyway, I came up to make sure and these were the words I heard him saying: 'Shelley,' he said, 'I swear by God Almighty that it's the truth I'm telling, the whole truth and nothing but the blasted truth, and if you believe me you're the fool I always took you for.' . . . And then he said . . . now what the divil was it he said?" Mrs. Kernan looked at Moxon for inspiration.

"Didn't he say some name?" Moxon was winking furiously.

"He did. Indeed he did. But for the life of me I can't recall it again—I know it was in the newspaper."

"Was it Twight?"

"It was Twight! He was saying at the top of his voice. 'Twight,' he said, 'you're a dirty dog, and if you don't lie down I swear I'll blow the bloody head off you!' I was certain he had taken leave of his senses; and it wasn't till afterwards, when the gentleman departed and I found the clipping under his head, that I realized what had been in his mind. It was a dreadful thing to be harbouring a man that had committed murder and made money out of it."

I said: "Just a moment, Mrs. Kernan. Did he know you had overheard him?"

Mrs. Kernan got up and flicked her ash into the fireplace. She was obviously at home in Moxon's room, and yet she did not seem at ease.

"He did. He was raving so much that I had to come up and put him to bed for fear he would disturb Mr. Moxon. Next morning, when I brought him his tea, he asked had I heard him saying anything strange. 'Divil I did!' I said, 'you were kicking up a terrible shindy and threatening to murder a dog called Twight. I never heard of a dog with a name like that!' That made him laugh—he had a terrible laugh, way up in his throat like the death-rattle itself. 'Mrs. Kernan,' he says, and his eyes were still laughing at me, 'I'm a very old man, in fact I'm senile, and my inside is in great disorder. For my part I'm prepared to let lying dogs sleep, but sometimes they start doggin' me again, and when they do I feel bound to remind them that I was the finest shot in Great Britain and Ireland, and that the crows are waiting for them as well as for me! Now have I made myself quite clear?' 'You have, Colonel,' I said. 'Sure you've made yourself as clear as Gregory's Mixture. And if you don't want to go to the dogs completely you'll do me and yourself a great favour by keeping off brandy for a while!' Next day he disappeared. And good riddance too, though he had a great way with him altogether. . . ."

She was in full flood. But Moxon soon cut her short. "Thank you, Mrs. Kernan. I think this gentleman has heard enough to convince him, and we don't want to keep you from your social engagements."

I thanked her too and she took herself off with surprising

promptitude, leaving a smell of cheap perfume in the room. I heard her hesitate on the landing, then run down the uncarpeted stairs making a noise like stage horsemen galloping 'off'.

"Well!" I said, when I was sure she had gone, "that certainly sounds like my man. I hope you won't think it impertinent if I ask one more question—do you think Mrs. Kernan's memory can be relied on about a conversation that took place six years ago? I noticed that she needed prompting over the name Twight."

Again I regretted that I couldn't see Moxon's eyes. But my question did not seem to embarrass him. On the contrary.

"Well done, Mr. Kennington, well done. I should have thought less of you if you had not put that question. But I can promise you that the conversation Mrs. Kernan has just described is substantially the one she reported to me the very day of Shelley's disappearance. I was so impressed by it at the time, so dubious about Mrs. Kernan's memory and my own as custodians of such historic words, that I took the trouble to note it down immediately and get Mrs. Kernan to verify my version. Perhaps you would care to see a copy?"

I thanked him and refused. I said: "I suppose the inference to be drawn from that conversation is that Millington-Forsett was still suffering from persecution mania dating from the libel action? He would have liked to take Twight's life, but he contented himself with taking his money instead?"

My imagination, fired by two large brandies, was working furiously on this theme and my tongue was longing for a good wag. But I had a bitter memory of my interview with Hodge, and I nearly choked myself trying not to be indiscreet.

"That's my own interpretation," Moxon was agreeing. "A man like Millington-Forsett, who has committed one murder and got away with it, is almost bound to be tempted again."

"Always assuming that he did really murder Travers, though in fact we have no right to suppose anything of the sort."

I was pleased with this judicial correction. But Moxon stared at me in astonishment.

"Mr. Kennington"—he spoke more in sorrow than in anger—"I understand that you cannot yet trust me well enough to be as frank with me as I am being with you. But you underrate me, Sir, you underrate me, and that is much harder to bear. Why did you bother to come and call on me if your essay about the Millington-Forsett trial is nothing but a harmless endorsement of the jury's verdict? I understood that it was in the nature of a revaluation, that you have even gone so far as to present new evidence?"

It was my turn to be astonished. "Really? I don't recall saying anything to give you that impression?"

"Oh come, Mr. Kennington, don't be so mysterious, so guarded. It makes it difficult for me to help you. Of course I know nothing of your essay but what anyone may read who goes to the Brixton Public Library and looks at Hodge and Ricketts's Christmas List. Having taken out one of your books, I could not but be curious to know more about this one, especially as I had had the pleasure of receiving a personal letter from you. As a matter of fact I was very struck by one or two phrases in your publisher's announcement— 'a scheming mind'—'charming but cold'—my dear Sir, I have only been waiting to tell you, from personal experience of your . . . er, hero, how very much I agree with you. And just because I have been close to him in the flesh, I am not in the least afraid to say that the man was the greatest villain unhanged. That was the general impression in England at the time of the trial, and now I am quite sure it was right. No, no, Mr. Kennington, let us face the fact that he was a murderer. But having said that, I for one will confess that I have always had a secret admiration for him—an admiration that only increased after he had robbed me. For me it is a privilege to have known such a man—cynical to the last, regretting nothing but the term put to his criminal career by old age and disease. Come, let us have one more drink and toast our wicked friend in the shades!"

Despite the winking, I was impressed by this speech. I even felt slightly ashamed of myself. When he raised his glass, I too drank solemnly. Then I raised my glass to Mr. Moxon.

"You have honoured his memory by being facetious," I said. "You appreciate his true worth. In his way he must have been a very brave man."

"Oh indeed, it takes great courage to hold the world in such contempt. He never said anything as though he expected to be taken seriously, and yet for that very reason people believed in him. I remember one day, when he was regaling me with his experiences in the French Foreign Legion, he described how his platoon had arrived to relieve a besieged fort in the desert only to find the fort full of dead men propped up with their rifles pointing through the slits, so as to give the enemy the impression that the defenders were still at their posts. The description was extraordinarily graphic, but I could not forbear to point out to him that it closely resembled an incident in a novel I had recently been reading. 'Why naturally,' he said, not at all disconcerted, 'it was I who told the story to the author.' 'Seriously?' I said. 'Yes, seriously. And that's what's really steep about it. You wouldn't think that an old man like me had ever been capable of saying boo to a goose!' "

"Was he facetious about his cancer too?"

"Oh, always, and particularly when he was in pain. He had a limerick about it. Let me see . . . ah yes:

> *There was an old warhorse called Shelley,*
> *Who managed to eat with no belly.*
> *When they said 'What a feat*
> *It must be to eat!'*
> *He replied 'The feat's calves' feets in jelly.' "*

I laughed, less at the limerick than at the thought of Millington-Forsett's coolness in choosing himself such a flippant alias. "He seems to have missed his vocation," I said. "Do you suppose he picked that alias because he had already made up the limerick and wanted it to be about himself?"

Moxon did not answer. He had been shaking with laughter himself; and my question, which caught him in a pause for drinking, set him off again so unexpectedly that his teeth rattled against the glass.

It was this curious tocsin—perhaps because I had already noticed Moxon's teeth with disapproval—which reminded me that night and fog were lying in wait for me beyond the dirty net curtains, and that it was high time for me to be going, before I became too elated.

I looked at my watch and drank up quickly. "You are going?" he said. "What a pity! But you have been more than kind to stay so long. May I hope that you will keep me informed about the progress of your enquiries?"

"Indeed you may. You have been very hospitable, and I can't tell you how much you have interested me."

"*Au revoir,*" he said. "You will excuse me if I don't come down—my lungs are not as sound as they were and I don't want to get fog in them."

64

CHAPTER FIVE

Foggy Romance

ALTHOUGH THE FOG was just as thick in Pimlico as it had been in Brixton, the atmosphere seemed much purer. After all, it was my native heath. Along the embankment cranes loomed, boats boomed, and mysterious blobs of red and green waxed and waned blearily to the accompaniment of swishing noises. Unshrouded, Pimlico streets were familiar and homely: shrouded, I thought them beautiful. Josephine would have said that this was illusion, ugliness veiled. But Josephine wasn't there, so what did it matter what she would have said?

Yet somehow it did matter. By the time I got home Mrs. Roddie's brother's pheasant was already in the oven, an all-pervading invitation to dinner, which reminded me that Josephine had haughtily declined my invitation. I hoped the larks' tongues would choke her.

But when the telephone rang I sprang downstairs, almost colliding with Mrs. Roddie, who was issuing massively from the kitchen, red-faced and spouting smoke.

"It'll be that *feemul* again," she panted. "She's been ringing every half hour since five and I'm fair sick of telling her you're out."

"Well, I'm not out now," I snarled, "and whether it was male or female you might have asked if there was any message."

As I removed the receiver I heard the tail-end of Mrs. Roddie's retort . . . "and you can tell her from me that I didn't get a wink of sleep this afternoon."

"Is that Mr. Kennington?" It was Josephine's office voice

without a trace of *sous-entendre.* "Will you hold the line a minute? Mr. Hodge wants to talk to you."

"Hullo, Kennington. I was wondering if you would by any chance be free for dinner tonight? I've got Ricketts and Miss Canning coming to share a scratch meal at my house and . . . you can't? Well, I don't blame you—wild horses wouldn't drag me out if I had a pheasant in the oven. But perhaps you could come round afterwards for a whiskey and soda? . . . Yes, I'm sure you've had a long day, but . . . yes, yes, the fog, filthy night, but if you do feel stronger after your pheasant we'd love to have you with us. We're all longing to hear . . . Oh all right then, we'll leave it at that. Come if you feel like it. Goodbye."

I banged down the receiver and called Josephine such a rude name that Mrs. Roddie, interpreting the conversation she had overheard as a stout fight against seduction, was finally convinced of my disabusement.

"Well, dear," she said consolingly, "you'll be better writing by your own fireside than gallivanting with the girruls." Then, to break the ice even she could feel forming between us: "Do you wish a wee drop of Oloroso to give you an appetite for the pheasant?"

My gastric juices were already in spate, but I accepted a measure of her sticky sherry just to show that I was a reformed character. When I had poured it down my bedroom basin I gave myself a stiff whiskey and sat down to lave my wounded pride. How *could* Josephine be so treacherous? . . . Unless . . . but no, her attitude towards Hodge had always seemed that of a loyal secretary . . . she could only have accepted Hodge's invitation, knowing that I was going to be invited too, out of pure desire to be revenged on me. I decided that I wouldn't go.

The pheasant was delicious, accompanied by bread sauce,

breadcrumbs done in pheasant-juice, and potatoes sliced in brown translucent slivers. As I ate through the enormous helping Mrs. Roddie had given me I reflected on the miracle that enabled this gaunt austere woman to cook so well while denying the claims of all other appetites. I told myself that such woman-bachelors would soon be an extinct race, but that Josephines were two a penny.

After dinner I reconsidered the Hodge invitation. My bottle of whiskey was completely empty, and I wanted more. But if I went round to the Jug and Bottle I would almost certainly become involved with the separated wife of an ex-colonial governor who was the nearest thing in nature to a grappling iron. Bad weather never put her off and she knew it didn't put me off either.

Reassuring Mrs. Roddie that I was only going 'round the corner', I walked to Victoria and took a taxi to Mecklenburg Square.

Bloomsbury in 1938 was rather like a cask of Napoleon brandy. It had been topped up so often that little remained but its reputation. But Hodge thought of himself as being a link between the old and the new. With the famous Christian names that he was apt to mention—Vanessa, Virginia, Maynard and Lytton—were mixed plain Johns and Henries whose surnames one could only guess because they appeared on Hodge and Ricketts books. It was my sense of having no interesting Christian name and not belonging to the Hodge circle that made me feel uncomfortable about going to Hodge's house for the first time.

"Surely you've seen all these before?" he said rather impatiently, as I lingered on the red-carpeted stairs examining the flight of book-jackets and poster-designs that went up the walls.

"They're fascinating," I said, "they make me feel as though I were in the Underground—one almost expects the stairs to move."

Since some of them were original designs by such artists as Vanessa Bell and Rex Whistler I suppose I had said the wrong thing. As we reached the landing, he said: "Here's something you'll appreciate as much as I do," and he pointed to the framed original of Josephine's jacket for *A Twist Somewhere*. "That girl's got a future as an artist—or she could have, if she gave up being my secretary."

My private opinion of this design was that Millington-Forsett himself could hardly have done more to prejudice the sale of the book. The figure in the centre was supposed to look morally deformed, but to me it only suggested an unfortunate tramp who had slipped a disk and been obliged to become a black-coated worker. However, there was no time for more than a passing pang of jealousy. Through an open door I could see Josephine sitting on a rug in front of the fire with her back against the leg of a spinet.

"Well," I said brightly, "this is a pleasure—I thought you were going to a City dinner this evening?"

"I was," she said, extending a row of lacquered fingers, "but I thought my mother would enjoy it more than I would. She's always complaining that my step-father takes me out and leaves her at home."

Ricketts, who was sitting in an armchair beside her, removed the pipe from his mouth and rose cumbrously to say hullo. The very sight of that low, sloping brow helped to put me at my ease. Even in his best pin-stripe suit he looked shaggy.

"Raymond," he said, directly as usual, "you're as thin as a rake. Either this sleuthing job is too much for you or you've fallen in love. Bachelors like you always fall like a ton of bricks."

"Well, *I* don't," I said, noticing for the first time what big feet he had, "I have Mrs. Roddie to look after me."

"But I gather you have Miss Canning as your assistant sleuth!"

He had now demonstrated that his mouth was quite big enough for him to put one of his big feet into. But recalling that without it he would never have been able to persuade Hodge to publish me, I entered into his little joke with all the malice I felt at that moment.

"Some hope! You know as well as I do that a good secretary always has to be in love with her boss!"

I had the impression that Hodge, who arrived at that moment with my drink, was not very much amused by my remark. Even less by Josephine's rejoinder. She stretched out her hands to the fire and leered at us over her shoulder: "Do go on. I am only a little piece of Dresden China waiting to belong to the highest bidder. But, *I can't bear being dropped!*"

Now neither of us was amused and I was relieved when Hodge adroitly changed the subject with a question that managed to preserve the mood.

"What news of Percy? You were so late in getting back that we were beginning to fear you had been knocked on the head. Wonderful publicity for your book of course, but then we should never have had the sequel."

As I talked I had the impression that they were all longing to say something. Ricketts cleaned and recleaned his pipe, while Hodge, who had been playing the spinet, couldn't get the music out of his fingers. I had scribbled down my conversation with Moxon and Mrs. Kernan on the way home in the bus and I could see they were impressed by the fullness of the report. Apart from exchanges of looks and one explosion from Ricketts when I quoted Millington-Forsett's limerick, they heard me out without a single comment.

Then Hodge said: "We're very grateful to you, Raymond. There's only one point I'd like to take up. Your interpretation of the 'dog Twight' episode, with which Moxon agreed, was that Millington-Forsett must have been suffering from persecution-mania? Right? Now, how do you reconcile that with what Patterson told you about Millington-Forsett and Twight conspiring together?"

I said: "Assuming that Shelley really was Millington-Forsett, and that he really said what Mrs. Kernan declares she overheard, then I don't think he was referring to the libel at all. It suggests to me that after the action was successfully staged, Twight tried to double-cross Millington-Forsett, or vice versa. But of course I couldn't tell Moxon what I really thought. Don't you see, it makes Twight's suicide more interesting?"

I had been looking forward to presenting this titbit as the principle fruit of my afternoon in Brixton. Though irrelevant to the main enquiry, the idea of a second murder—one that Scotland Yard had apparently not suspected—had been steadily growing in my mind, and I intended it to sound sensational.

Hodge merely grunted. "Fascinating idea," he said, "but what interests us now is that Millington-Forsett probably double-crossed Twight. That sounds far more likely than the persecution-complex theory, and it makes Mrs. Kernan's story seem more credible. But what do you think about it all yourself? Did Moxon manage to convince you that Shelley really was Millington-Forsett?"

"Absolutely. As I've told you, I tried hard not to be convinced. I was thoroughly suspicious about the whole set-up.

What finally did it was the Shelley limerick. I'm prepared to bet anything you like that the man who made up that limerick was the same man who, in the middle of his trial for murder, had the face to write a note to a fashionable lady in court, complimenting her on her hat. Her name was Mary Mitton and she was evidently an old flame. She showed the note to a reporter afterwards:

> *Dear Mary. my friend in all weathers,*
> *Though I find myself sat in the dock,*
> *It cheers me to see you in feathers*
> *Admiring—your faithful—'old cock'."*

"Wonderful!" said Ricketts. "The chap was an Elizabethan, no worse than Marlowe or probably Shakespeare for that matter. What a book he could have written!"

Hodge said: "More in the Cavalier tradition, I would say— gay and completely unscrupulous, but judging from his poems I don't think he would have been a Hodge and Ricketts author. Well now, Miss Canning"—he turned to Josephine, who had sat completely silent through this conversation— "what about giving him our little item of news?"

Josephine said: "You remember Mr. Hodge suggested this morning that I should go to Somerset House again? Well, I did, and this time I struck lucky. I found a Percy Shelley who died in 1933 in Marylebone Hospital—of stomach cancer. I happen to know Dick Burton, who's one of the governors of the hospital, and he gave me permission to go and look up their records. This Shelley apparently had no money or relatives and he was about the same age as Millington-Forsett. But the fact that seems really conclusive is that the Matron remembers him as an old rolling-stone, *who told stories about the Foreign Legion* and made them all laugh even when he was dying."

She looked pleased with herself, and I was not sure it suited her. For a moment I could say nothing: it had never occurred to me that we would trace him so easily. I had a sense of anticlimax which had something to do with Josephine.

"Well," I said at last, "that seems to be that. I must say I'm rather sorry!"

"Sorry! But good God, man, don't you want your book to come out? We do, anyway."

"Of course I'm glad in that way. But I know so much more about Millington-Forsett now, that the original essay no longer satisfies me: it seems, well—just a piece of journalism, already out of date."

"Nevertheless"—it was Ricketts this time—"it's a damn good book and we want it to come out right away. When the sequel comes, and then the sequel to the sequel, it will send your readers right back to *A Twist Somewhere* and your books with Millington-Forsett in them will sell like a string of sausages."

I said: "All right, but don't let's be in too much of a hurry. I've still to be completely convinced that the Shelley who died in Marylebone Hospital is the one who lived in Crick Street, Brixton. Before I agree to go ahead I want to try and get corroboration from Mrs. Danby."

Ricketts said: "The trouble with Raymond is, he's enjoying his new career so much he can't bear to give it up."

But Hodge said: "I agree with him, really. *We've* no right to be convinced until *he* is, and anyway there's no harm in making assurance doubly sure."

Ricketts groaned: "He'd better make it snappy, that's all I've got to say. What about all those poor kids who have written to Father Christmas—I want to put *A Twist Somewhere* in their stockings!"

Josephine was looking so sphinx-like that I stirred myself

and said: "Miss Canning seems to have something on her mind."

She put her hand over her mouth and yawned, looking at me over the tips of her fingers.

"Now what *could* a working girl have on her mind at a quarter past midnight?"

"Men," Ricketts suggested promptly.

"No, bed," said Josephine. "I have to get up early and finish off that jacket design for Mrs. Sulzburger's memoirs—she's descending upon us tomorrow morning."

I found myself in the street with Ricketts and Josephine. The fog was so thick we couldn't see the edge of the pavement and Ricketts's car was a lifeless hulk stranded in the middle of nowhere. We groped our way to Hyde Park Corner, where Josephine asked Ricketts to drop her.

"I'll get out here too," I said. "I could do with a bit of a walk."

As Ricketts drove away, Josephine said: "Well, what are we going to do now?"

"Do? I'm going to see you home. Don't you live somewhere near Shepherd's Market?"

"I do. But I don't feel in the least like going home. Let's go to the Miranda and have a drink."

"It's too late and you're tired. Besides, isn't the Miranda a nightclub? I hate dancing, and what's more important, I haven't any money on me."

"That," said Josephine, "is plain enough to put most girls off. But I feel like talking to you and I happen to be the type of female that always gets her own way. Taxi!"

"It's engaged. We haven't a hope."

"Then we'll walk. It's only just round the corner in Mayfair and from there I only have to stagger a few steps into bed."

She was already dragging me across the concrete flats of Hyde Park Corner, patchily visible in the flickering of flares. When I protested she said: "If you open your mouth you'll get fog down your throat, so you'd much better come quietly."

I have always detested nightclubs. I dislike being forced to pay through the nose for expensive titbits one has no appetite for, just for the privilege of quenching one's thirst: I am depressed by the spectacle of tired couples jigging about on a floor the size of a postage stamp because they can't keep still or go to bed. I disapprove of the lack of gaiety—due, I suspect, to the places being frequented by people with a surfeit of money and leisure. But I was so flattered by the argument Josephine now produced that I went along like a lamb.

I had fallen back on my last defence, that I had no money, when Josephine stopped and said: "Look here, it's no good arguing with me about things that don't matter. I'm a trivial girl, I have plenty of money, and as far as I can see in this fog, I've no other means of getting you into my power than by carrying you off and making you thoroughly embarrassed."

It was a stuffy little place, in the bowels of Mayfair, but dim and listless enough to be restful. The floor was made of cubes of coloured glass lit from below, and during the dancing there was no other light but the red lamp on the white piano, which picked out the hands of a black man playing blue music. The dancers walked around in a kind of dream, and the almost invisible occupants of the other tables round the floor talked in low voices, as though afraid of waking the somnambulists.

"Do you come here often?" I asked Josephine, thinking of the aristocratic name she had flung as a sop to the Cerberus at the door.

"I use it for talking," she said, adding with emphasis, "for

74

intimate conversations. It's an ideal place for being private in public—one can be indiscreet without being compromised."

When we had settled about drinks she suddenly said: "What I'm dying to know is the real reason why you reacted as you did when you heard Millington-Forsett was dead?"

"Oh, I don't know. I suppose Ricketts was right: I had been keyed up by the afternoon in Brixton. Things were getting more and more exciting, then, plop! the fun was suddenly over . . . I told you the other reason."

"Yes, but I wasn't convinced by it. I expected you to heave a sigh of relief, not so much because you were out of the Millington-Forsett wood, but because the Canning danger was averted!"

"The Canning danger?"

"Yes, you can't stand females, can you—even as collaborators?"

"Who said I couldn't? As a matter of fact you're quite wrong. One of the reasons for my disappointment was the thought that our little collaboration was over."

"But you didn't think I was any good, did you? You had hardly asked me before you began to regret it?"

"It wasn't that at all. I had begun to fear that it might involve dirty work."

"And if it had? Why should you have minded?"

She went on inexorably till finally I gave in and said: "I didn't want to . . . the fact is . . . well, if you must know, I began to realize that you were more interesting as a woman than as a Watson. The two might have gone together if you had thought the same about me. But you don't. You only think of me as an intriguing novelty, because I live in Pimlico, didn't go to a Public School, and because at the moment I happened to be picking over some rather interesting bones. We're at cross-purposes, aren't we?"

"Look, Raymond," she said, "if you knew the first thing about women you would realize that we don't keep things apart like that. It's true that you're different from my other friends, but I don't see only the surface differences. You're real. You live in the world as it is. And you know yourself— at least I *think* you do, though how can I be certain, when you won't let me get anywhere near you, when you just don't believe in women?"

"But I do believe in women. That's why I'm still a bachelor. The trouble is I've got ideas far above my station: I don't want to be involved with second-rate women—for more than one night anyway—and the first-rate ones. . . . Oh hell, what am I talking about? But you're right about my knowing myself: I know I'm too selfish for any enduring relationship. I find it hard enough looking after myself without having to look after somebody else as well. And . . . well, I just enjoy living alone, that's all."

"Is that really all? I mean, don't you sometimes bite your fingernails and long?"

"Sometimes. But solitude might be worse with two."

She touched my hand lightly and I understood that the worst was over. She had got what she wanted.

"Shall we dance a bit? I adore dancing with reluctant men —they always have so much more to say for themselves."

I said: "All right. You'll be the first girl whose clutches I have ever walked into with open eyes. You'll be lucky if you only get your toes trodden on."

"Don't worry," she said, "I'm quite capable of looking after myself."

About three in the morning I came out of my amorous swoon with the definite impression that Josephine really was capable of looking after herself. She was tough enough to get involved with on a temporary basis. I might have lost my grip on reality entirely, if I had not had it as a basic article of my scepticism that girls like Josephine do not marry men like me.

We ended up curiously sober and gay, considering how much we had drunk, making urgent plans for spinning out the Millington-Forsett adventure. She too seemed to realize that he was the old pander to whom we owed everything.

"I'm going to prove that Claude Nevil murdered Twight," I announced, "even if it means going to Paris."

"And if it does mean going to Paris," said Josephine, "you're not going to leave me behind."

I kissed her on the doorstep of her parents' house, and she submitted, I thought, with more grace than enthusiasm. For a moment we stood wrapped in silence and fog that was like the taste of ashes in the mouth. She whispered a soft goodnight and brushed my face with a scented glove. Then, as though alarmed to find me less reluctant than she had thought, and anxious to send me away in the right frame of mind: "What *could* you have meant by 'second-rate women'? You must have been talking to Mrs. Roddie!"

CHAPTER SIX

Mrs. Danby lets the Cat out of the Bag

I DREAMT that I had received a threatening letter from Millington-Forsett warning me that I was a marked man and that if I loved Josephine I had better give her up immediately. It was bliss to wake and realize that he was dead, yet sufficiently immortal to keep Josephine and me together for a while, in a dark passage of his past.

After the conversation in Hodge's flat I decided to go and see Mrs. Danby quickly. Though she probably wouldn't be able to confirm his death, I had a vague hope that she might throw some light on the Twight mystery. And anyway, unless I bungled the interview, I could hardly help learning *something* of interest.

I rang her up, this time not in fear and trembling, but in the calm assurance that the sting had been drawn out of that family and that I was in a stronger position to do the talking.

She had checked up on me since our last telephone conversation. She remembered distinctly who I was. When I said I had important news for her she softened up sufficiently to ask me to tea, adding—rather charmingly, I thought—"You'd better buy some butter and buns on the way. You see, I never go out in this sort of weather."

I bought butter and buns in the Fulham Road and at four o'clock precisely I presented myself at Mrs. Danby's door, in a large block of Council flats.

The first thing that struck me as she opened it was an overpowering stench of cat. Mrs. Danby had one perched on her shoulder and the sight of the paper bag in my hand provoked a chorus of mewing from at least half a dozen others dispersed round the little room on chairs and cushions. She introduced me to them with a graceful sweep of her hand—"Mr. Pennington, these are my Pussies—Pussies, this is Mr. Pennington . . . I'm sorry—*Kennington*—I keep confusing you with the young man who did the Caesarian on poor Emily. Get up, Emily, and give the young man a chair."

So saying, she scooped up Emily with one hand and relieved me of my bag of buns with the other. "Oh, good egg! You've brought six. Now we shall all be happy!"—and to my astonishment she took four of the buns and began to feed them to the cats, which growled and hissed at one another as they retired into corners, each with a piece.

"It's so difficult to feed the family," she complained, "when the weather is too bad to go out."

The smell was nauseating. "Do you mind if I smoke?" I asked, firmly taking out my cigarette-case.

"Of course not. My husband smoked like a chimney." She hurried over to open a window. "That's better now. You can talk to the cats for a minute while I go and get the tea."

While she was in the kitchenette I took a look at the gallery of photographs on the mantelpiece. There were so many of them that they overlapped. One, framed in silver, seemed to have the place of honour. It showed a very handsome boy in a sailor suit with a fishing rod and basket on his knees; a girl leant over him with one arm round his shoulders and a hand resting on the arm of his chair. It seemed incredible that that pretty little thing, with carefully done ringlets and flirtatious eyes, should have turned into the fat untidy old lady with straggling grey hair and glasses mended with sticking-plaster. Yet something about the mouth made me sure it was her, and I was equally sure that the insolent, amused eyes of the boy belonged to Claude Nevil Millington-Forsett. '*A Twist Some-where*,' I was thinking, 'and it must have happened very early.' By the time Mrs. Danby returned with the tea I was making polite conversation to Emily, who was washing herself on my lap.

"Ah, you like her," she said dotingly, "and I can see she likes you—she's most particular about the laps she patronizes."

When she poured out the tea, from a brown pot with a broken spout, she bent her head and looked sharply at me over the rims of her glasses, as though sizing me up for the first time.

"Well now, Mr. Pennington, I must tell you frankly that the first time you rang me up I didn't like your voice at all— I thought you were one of those odious Twights trying to make money out of my family misfortune. My second thought was that you had lent Nevil money and wanted to get it back from me—oh, don't smile; I have suffered more from so-called friends of his than I have from all the journalists. He was always a prey to unscrupulous people—generous, you know, and very easily led. . . . No, don't say anything till I've finished. . . . Well, I found out about you from my little bookseller in the Kings Road, and it seems that though you do write about crime, you are a respectable author and you have some regard for truth. That's why I've decided to help you. I know you are writing about my brother and now I've seen you I believe you may be the right man to clear away the horrible suspicion that has always rested on him—despite the clear verdict at the trial. . . ."

I was beginning to wriggle with embarrassment and I made one more attempt to speak. Again she shut me up:

"Before I tell you *anything* about my brother I want to know if you have any news of him. It is a strange thing that though we were very close when we were young and I was the only member of the family who stood by him in the old days, I haven't seen or heard of him since 1932. You see, while my husband was alive I wasn't even allowed to speak of him, and after George's death it was too late—he had been so persecuted, you know, that he had to live under false names, and he had got so into the habit of mistrusting everybody that he believed I had turned against him too. He *never* gave me his address, and if he wanted to get in touch with me, he used to send intermediaries—unpleasant men who said they were his friends and sooner or later always asked for money. But they never got any." . . . Mrs. Danby suddenly looked vague. Her pale blue eyes seemed to disappear and she repeated the last phrase twice, adding with emphasis, "No, not a penny." Then, gazing round the apathetic audience of cats, as though she were expecting them to confirm it: "We couldn't spare any, could we, pussies?"

I took advantage of this lapse. "Mrs. Danby, when you last saw him, was he well?"

Her eyes focussed and she looked at me again over the top of her spectacles: "He was just out of hospital, where he had been treated for cancer. But the doctors told him he might live to be eighty. He said he had never felt better in his life. . . . Oh, Mr. Pennington, I see what you mean . . . you've come to tell me he's dead, haven't you?"

I inclined my head and waited for a moment in respectful silence, while she gazed into the fire, caressing the grey tabby on her lap with swift expert head-to-tail strokes. Presently she said: "And to think that he never sent for me . . . that he preferred to die quite alone!" She took off her glasses and wiped her eyes with a none-too-clean handkerchief. "He was a proud man, Mr. Pennington. When I asked him if he was really all right, do you know what he said to me? 'Kate,' he said, 'I'm like a cat with nine lives: each one lasts ten years, and I've just had my eighth. I'm going to live to be ninety, you'll see. I'm not too old to have some fun!' Tell me, where and when did he die?"

I told her all I thought she ought to know, which was precious little. When I had finished she said: "Thank you, Mr. Pennington. I shall go to the hospital and find out where he is buried. I shall put red carnations on his grave. He always loved red carnations. When he was young he never went out without one in his buttonhole. My father used to say it wasn't manly, but then Father never approved of Nevil. I've often thought that if he hadn't been so strict with him, he wouldn't have been such a wild boy."

"Is that him in the silver frame?" I asked. "I recognized *you* as soon as I saw it."

She nodded, and for a moment we both stared up at the mantelpiece. Then she said: "What a handsome boy he was! And of course he knew it! That was the trouble. He thought he could get round anybody by just looking at them. He once said to me: 'Katie, we're a pretty good-looking pair, aren't we? What a pity we're poor, and brother and sister. But never mind, we're both going to be millionaires!' Life was very cruel to him, Mr. Pennington . . ."

She appeared to be going off into another reverie, so I encouraged her by saying: "Judging from that photograph, he knew how to laugh at life."

"That's right, how well you understand him! He did laugh at life, and at death too. In fact he used to frighten me sometimes."

"How, Mrs. Danby?"—I still felt like a worm, but having wriggled so far into her confidence, I told myself I would be a fool not to get all I could.

"Although we were very fond of each other we had terrible quarrels. Sometimes, if I refused to say I was sorry, he would threaten to kill himself. He did it so often that I decided he was only trying to frighten me, and the next time he said he was going to shoot himself I said: 'Go on. I bet you won't do it!' He loaded his little four-ten gun and presented it at his temple, putting his finger on the trigger. 'Now,' he said, 'do you still dare me?' 'No, I don't,' I said. 'Please, Nevil, put that thing away, and I'll promise never to be horrid again.' I never had such a fright in my life—I really believe he would have done it."

"Do you mean he would have done it just to pay you out, or because he really wanted to die?"

"Oh, he didn't want to die at all. He just liked playing with fire. He had a very funny sense of humour."

"Morbid, do you mean?"

"You might call it morbid, I suppose. As a young man he was always talking about ways of dying. He invented a game —a sort of Consequences—in which each player had to imagine he was going to kill himself. You first thought of a reason why you were tired of life, then you wrote it down and passed it on: the next person had to write a suitable suicide letter, and the last had to describe how the body was found. I know it sounds terribly morbid, but the results were often very funny, and we didn't play in a morbid spirit."

"It was just a game"—I encouraged her—"like Hide and Seek or . . . or Murders?" I could feel the pulse beating in my temple, but I stroked the cat and tried to make my next question sound casual: "Did he ever talk of suicide afterwards? Life must have seemed much less amusing to him later, at the time of the trial and all that publicity?"

"Well, as a matter of fact he did once. It was shortly after he had been acquitted. He told me that if it hadn't been for my believing in him he wouldn't have thought twice about killing himself. Being acquitted of murder was almost as bad as being condemned, he said, but suicide would be taken as an admission of guilt. The really dreadful part of the whole thing was the attitude of his family—they would have absolutely nothing to do with him from that day onwards. My father cut him out of his will, my brothers pretended that it would ruin their careers to have him in their houses, and my mother, who would have stood by him through thick and thin, was already in her grave before he came to trial."

"You surely don't mean they thought him guilty?"

"Oh, I don't know. Of course they *said* he was innocent, but because they weren't convinced in their souls, as I was, they couldn't make him feel that they believed. *You don't think he was guilty, do you, Mr. Pennington?*"

It was the most embarrassing moment of my life. I had been dreading it throughout the whole interview. But in a way I was glad not to have to pretend any more.

"Mrs. Danby, I *do* believe he did it. But that is only on the available evidence. I feel there was so much that never came out at the trial."

"Oh!" she said. "Oh, how horrible! You have been sitting there all this time, allowing me to think you were on my side, *our* side. And now that he is dead, nobody can stop you saying it. . . . Well, what are you waiting for? Why don't you go?"

I put the cat down gently and got up. My legs were unsteady, and though I knew perfectly well what I wanted to say I hadn't the face to say it—until Mrs. Danby thought fit to address the cats:

"We never liked his voice, did we, Pussies? We always thought he wasn't a gentleman. . . ."

"Mrs. Danby," I said, "you can't stop me writing what I've already written. But your bookseller was right. I do care for the truth. And if you can tell me anything that would help me to believe in his innocence I promise I will publish it afterwards and do all in my power to make amends."

She went over to the window and shut it with a bang.

"I have nothing to say to you, Mr. Pennington. You and your creatures can do what you like."

The smell of that tea-party lingered in my nostrils, embarrassing and persistent as civet. If Mrs. Danby had played her cards right, she might have succeeded in sealing my lips about her brother, at any rate till her death. It had been in my mind several times that I had no right to hurt the old lady and that it was not in fact too late to substitute another essay, even at the risk of alienating Hodge and Ricketts. But she had finished by clawing me where it hurt, and now I felt no compunction whatever. As soon as I got home I rang up Hodge and told him he could safely go ahead with the publication of *A Twist Somewhere*. I also informed him that I was going to Paris for a few days 'to see about a cat Mrs. Danby has let out of the bag'. I told him I would leave my address with Miss Canning.

"What's all this about your going to Paris and leaving your address with me?"

Josephine, in full warpaint, stood waiting for me as I came through the door of the bar. She beckoned me imperiously into a corner where she had already established herself with *The Times* Crossword and some sherry.

"But you didn't really mean that you wanted to come too? It's the sort of thing people always say at three in the morning."

"When *I* say things at three in the morning, I mean them. I'm never properly awake until after midnight and I wouldn't be as awake as I am at this moment if I didn't suspect you of trying to double-cross me again."

"Josephine," I said, "if I look meek, it's because my manners are good. But I won't be hag-ridden, henpecked or beguiled. If you come to Paris with *me*, you will come on my terms, after telling your parents and making your peace with Hodge. Now is that understood?"

She had a large mouth you couldn't possibly take seriously until she smiled. Then you weren't quite sure whether she had already fed, or whether you were destined to be the next victim.

"All right," she said, smiling, "when do we start?"

"*I* am starting tomorrow morning. Whether you start or not depends on whether you can satisfy me that I shall not be pursued for debauching a minor, or alienating the affections of a secretary."

"Well, to begin with, I have reached the age of consent. Secondly, my stepfather couldn't care less. Thirdly, my mother, who thinks very freely, brought me up to look out for myself and to tell her all. Fourthly, tomorrow is Friday and I'm due for a long weekend. As for my affections for Mr. Hodge, they're not of the sort you could possibly alienate, however much you flatter yourself."

"So far, so good. But you must also satisfy me that you have friends and relations in Paris, with whom you can easily establish contact."

"My step-uncle is Counsellor at the British Embassy and he absolutely dotes on me. So that's settled. Now about you. Do you want me as Josephine or Miss Canning?"

I considered this delicate question for a minute. Then I said: "Thank you, I'll have it white. I want to get some sleep while I'm there. You said you liked reluctant men, didn't you?"

"I do. I just wanted to be quite sure you really were the sort of man my mother would approve of me going to Paris with!"

86

The bar we were sitting in was a comfortable unpretentious place in Wardour Street, which, apart from its shellfish and Muscadet, had strong associations for me with that famous Oyster Bar 'in the immediate neighbourhood of Leicester Square', patronized by Prince Florizel of Bohemia. I mentioned this to Josephine and was delighted to find that she knew her Stevenson. I laid bare all my enthusiasm. I discoursed at length on Stevenson's style, his ability to make the fantastic credible, the excitement it still gave me to reread the stories I was brought up on. She led me on, and in my innocence I began to feel that she was more than attractive: she was a soul-mate. Then suddenly she turned upon me.

"Do you know, I suspected you from the very beginning of being the sort of man who *would* revel in Stevenson—men without women, having glorious adventures all over the world without any domestic responsibilities, yet sustained all the time by the memory of some pure, uncomplicated damsel tirelessly longing by the fireside at home!"

Josephine was one of those sophisticated girls for whom sex-warfare on the guerilla scale is a technique for probing the strength of the male defences. Her attacks, even when direct, were never intended to wound. But this time, despite the humour of her mouth and eyes, I had a feeling that she was more in earnest than she realized herself, and my reaction was all the more sensitive because I didn't think she cared enough about me to be bitter.

"From the point of view of feminine nature I suppose all men are a bit eccentric. Bachelors—even unconfirmed ones —must seem completely crazy. But you were thinking of somebody else, weren't you?"

She looked surprised and rather troubled: "Was I really thinking of somebody else? If so, it was *à propos* of you. . . ."

"Will you tell me about him?"

"Sometime. But not now. . . . I must start training to be Miss Canning. What happened with Mrs. Danby?"

I told her about Mrs. Danby, leaving out nothing but the remark with which she had sent me packing: I didn't feel like repeating that. When I had finished she said: "There, I told you so! I always said you were wrong about his background. Abnormal backgrounds just weren't recognized in those days. Now you'll have to bring psychology into the story—ha! But I can't see how this suicide fixation of Millington-Forsett's helps your theory that he murdered Twight—unless of course you've been holding out on me again?"

I said: "You didn't give me time to tell you that I spent the morning in the Newspaper Room at Hendon looking up the Twight suicide."

As I was opening the school exercise book in which I had copied out the extracts I wanted, I caught Miss Canning giving me one of her Josephine looks, personal and penetrating.

"I love your notebooks," she said, "you always have so many, don't you? I'm glad you haven't got a briefcase. I couldn't bear it if you looked shiny and professional!"

Most of the English dailies of the time had printed something about Twight's death, under such headlines as Libel Man Had No Luck and British Journalist Ends Life in Seine. But either they were afraid of Millington-Forsett (as Patterson had alleged) or they had ceased to be interested in a shady colleague who no longer had any news value. The nearest thing to a story was from the Paris correspondent of the *News Telegraph* printed several days after the 'tragedy'.

In the early hours of Monday Morning M. Jean Moineau,

lockkeeper at the Seine barrage near Melun, was called out to let a barge pass up the river. He was winding up the sluice-gate when he was horrified to see an arm float palm-uppermost from under the plank-bridge he was standing on. The arm belonged to the fully-clothed body of a corpulent middle-aged man which had been pressed against the lockgates by the current and partly submerged by the undertow. A doctor, hastily summoned to the spot, believed that the man had fallen into the river when drunk: he had been dead many hours.

Examination of the dead man's papers have enabled the police to identify him as J. T. Twight, a London journalist recently in the news as co-defendant in a libel action brought by Mr. C. N. Millington-Forsett. He had been in Paris for some weeks writing articles for a Sunday newspaper.

Subsequent enquiries at a bar he frequented in the Saint-Germain-des-Prés Quarter of Paris established the fact that Twight had been suffering from nervous depression, aggravated by habitual heavy drinking. They have now led to the discovery of a letter written to a lady, in which he announced his intention to take his life. Interrogated today by police officers the lady has confirmed the theory of suicide. An unhappy love-affair seems to have been the decisive, if not the only motive.

The following Sunday the *Sunday Globe* came out with a sensational story by a Staff Reporter. It was printed round a large photograph of Twight wearing a tweed suit and a Tyrolese hat, and began by describing him as 'a genial lover of humanity'. As one read on, it soon became apparent that the article was not so much a white-washing of Twight as an attempt to white-wash the *Sunday Globe* for employing such a scandal-monger, and to boost the sales of the numbers containing his last articles.

His pen was at the service of a wide public, and I am proud to reveal that after his reputation had been severely damaged by the Millington-Forsett libel action the *Sunday Globe* alone, of all the national Sunday newspapers, continued to recognize the idealism that made him ruthless in exposing all that is corrupt and shabby in our national life.

The *Sunday Globe* sent him to Paris because he, of all English journalists, seemed best equipped to paint a true picture of the social sickness behind the recent political scandals in France.

The writer now got down to the real business, which was to make a story out of Twight's suicide that millions of readers would be able to enjoy over their fried bread and bacon.

It was surely by one of Fate's strangest whims that this experienced writer and man of the world should have found the love of his life at the moment when he was engaged in collecting material about the organization of commercialized sex. I knew Twight. I did not believe the reports that he had died of a broken heart. I went to Paris, and since he apparently had no relatives concerned about his fate, I went on behalf of this newspaper to get the truth and bring it home. By the courtesy of the police I was allowed to see Twight's last letter and to pursue my enquiries independently.

The next paragraph was mysteriously headed HE DIED WRITING.

Here is the letter, unmistakably in Twight's hand. It

concerns a girl whom I have seen and spoken to. But it also concerns thousands of readers who have read Twight's writings and will recognize the purest paragraphs he ever wrote:

My love,

By the time you receive this, if you ever do, I will have crossed the Great Divide into the Cold Region. I shall be out of my misery. The heart that was yours, though you spurned it, will have become indifferent to fleshly ends. But if you ever meant any of the things you said to me when I was in your arms, I hope that this last, desperate movement of the pen I have lived by in the service of Truth, will stir some warmth in those ashes. The rest is silence.

John Twight

I read this letter to Josephine without putting any comment in my voice. Her reaction was as categoric as I had hoped.

"Nobody could possibly write like that on the verge of suicide. Nobody in love could write like that—not even J. T. Twight."

"Yet Twight wrote it. There seems to be no doubt about that."

"Then he wrote it for . . ." As the thought struck her, she whistled softly. "You mean he wrote it for the Suicide Game?"

"It might be, mightn't it? When I first read the letter I half thought it might be genuine false emotion, if you see what I mean. The article it's embedded in is so phony that it seems almost genuine by comparison. And then I didn't see how it could be forgery. But when Mrs. Danby mentioned the Suicide Game . . ."

"And yet the police were convinced, weren't they?"

"Apparently. But put yourself in their place, knowing nothing of Twight's criminal activities and thinking of him as a drunken English journalist involved in an *affaire passionelle*. Paris is the climate for that sort of thing. They're always fishing foreigners out of the Seine. How can anybody say the letter is false when every circumstance points to its being authentic?"

"But the writer of the article says he knew him and he seems to have been satisfied?"

"It suited his paper and it suited him to find that Twight died in the throes of a beautiful passion. Now listen to the bit about the girl. . . .

I telephoned Mademoiselle X at a Montparnasse Hotel. To my surprise she seemed eager to meet me. 'Oh,' she said, with only a trace of a French accent, 'it will be nice to see anybody from England. My mother was English, you see.'

I was prepared to find a voluptuous siren. I found a pretty brunette in her twenties, dressed simply and tastefully in black. 'It was a terrible shock,' she told me. 'You see, I was helping him all the time with his work.' When I asked her if she realized how much he had loved her, her candid brown eyes became misty. 'Of course I knew he loved me, but what could I do?—I thought of him as a good friend. I wanted to help him overcome his weakness; for the English—you will excuse me—do not drink wisely. But I suppose I only made things worse for him. Oh, it was terrible being questioned by the police—they treated me like a *fille*, how do you say it?—a bad woman. You were a friend of his, weren't you? Will you believe me when I tell you that I broke with him for his own good, for the sake of his work, and his . . . future?'

What could I say? I looked round the room. Books and fresh flowers gave an intimate touch. My eyes fell on the bed, and suddenly I felt ashamed that I had come to accuse this girl of betraying my friend. How could I judge the strange ways of the human heart?

I left with my list of unasked questions. As I crossed the lovely bridge that joins the artist's side of the river to the historic palace of the French kings I tore up my paper and threw it into the shining river on whose mercy John Twight had cast himself in his despair. . . .

There was a cynical leer in my voice as I finished and I was surprised to find Josephine wasn't entirely with me.

"Poor devil! Whatever happened to him, he didn't deserve that slushy epitaph. . . . Of course the girl couldn't have been like that really. She must have been a smalltime Delilah."

"Exactly. I believe she was *cast for the part of Delilah* in the tragedy Twight wrote for himself—unwittingly. Production by Claude Nevil Millington-Forsett."

"But have we any evidence that Millington-Forsett ever went to Paris?"

"Of course we haven't—yet. Though we have Bairstow's statement that a year or so after Twight's death he had 'business relations' with the continent."

Josephine shrugged her shoulders lightly. "When one knows so little about a person, and the little one knows is all so ghastly, the tendency is to invest him with 'superior evil'—wasn't that the phrase you used to describe your sensations walking up Crick Road, Brixton, in the fog? . . . By the way, Ricketts wants to give a cocktail party for the publication of *A Twist Somewhere*. He thinks Moxon should be asked and everybody else who's helped you, except Mrs. Danby of course, to meet reviewers and give the thing a real send-off!"

"What a child that man is!" I said, "and how adroitly you always manage to change the subject just when we're getting down to brass tacks!"

"Coffin-nails," said Josephine. "I didn't mean to change the subject. I just lack concentration, like most women."

CHAPTER SEVEN

Getting Warm in Paris

IT WASN'T UNTIL we were actually in Paris that I shook off the effects of the Channel crossing. Then the cold air, the yapping of the traffic, and the cries of the news-sellers affected me like a series of therapeutic slaps in the face. I sat up and registered the blaze of cafés and neon-signs, suddenly attuned to the universal mood of impatience and caprice which our taxi expressed in every fibre of its ancient body. We came to some traffic lights and the driver, who had been shouting '*eh alors?*' every time his reckless career was checked, suddenly accelerated, then braked violently in the middle of a crossing: amid shrill whistles, the ineffectual shouts of the *agent* on point-duty, and the protests of an overburdened bus, which hooted and waved an illuminated arm.

We picked ourselves up and smiled experimentally.

"Hullo!" said Josephine, in a voice that struck me as ominously tender, and immediately started putting on fresh warpaint.

At our hotel the night-porter was already on duty—a wine-faced little man with drooping moustaches, wearing an apron and a striped linen jacket with brass buttons.

"*Mais oui, monsieur,*" he said. "Would you like a double or two single beds?"

"Two single rooms," I said, embarrassed. Then, annoyed by Josephine's broad uninhibited smile: "As you can see from our passports."

"Communicating?" he suggested understandingly.

"No, there's no necessity for that, thank you."

He shrugged his shoulders and looked puzzled: "*Eh bien, tant pis! On n'est jeune qu'une fois!*"

Josephine looked up from the blotter on which she had been doodling little ostriches with their heads buried in the sand. "The monsieur was never young—at least not since I've known him!"

After that I disliked myself a little. But as I told her afterwards—and all the more firmly because I suspected her of having forgotten—"Those were the terms of the contract, weren't they?"

"Of course they were," she said. "I never wanted anything else, but you don't have to express panic at the very thought of it!"

Our hotel was in a little street in the triangle between the Boulevard Raspail and the Rue de Rennes, not far from Notre-Dame-des-Champs. Washed and changed, we plunged into this Mecca of the long-haired men and the short-haired girls who lurked all day creating things in sordid bedrooms, and came forth at night under the rosy sky of Montparnasse to while away the hours in bars and *bals musettes*.

Josephine had attended a life-drawing class at the *Grande Chaumière* before going into Hodge and Ricketts, and she was all for initiating me right away into the artistic night-life of the quarter. But I said firmly that I thought criminals could be just as colourful as artists: "Why don't we combine business with pleasure and try and find out the bar Twight patronized?"

We were already walking briskly, arm-in-arm, in the direction of Saint-Germain-des-Prés, and at this proposal Josephine braked violently.

"I don't want to seem callous after that crossing. But I don't think I could face a pub-crawl in quest of Twight with my belt hanging round my backbone! Could you bear to have dinner first?"

She had so arranged things that I was standing on an iron

grating in the pavement, my nose subjected to a powerful aroma of cooking; while at eye level a row of thick silhouettes, wiping their chops behind muslin curtains, suggested that if I didn't make up my mind quickly, there would be nothing left to eat at all.

"Quick," she said, taking me resolutely by the hand, "it's kidneys being done in red wine. But I warn you I shall want to begin with soup and *hors d'œuvres*. . . ."

After dinner we set off in high spirits. We were at our fourth bar, slightly drunk and very discouraged that nobody had ever heard of Twight or Millington-Forsett, when an American who had been standing us drinks said: "Hey, why don't you try Charley's Bar in the Rue des Cannettes? I guess you'll meet some odd fish there, and I believe Charley himself is some sort of an Englishman—ex-welter-weight champion, knocked out by Pugnier in the tenth round in 1926. . . ."

The Rue des Cannettes was a mean, ill-lit street just off the Place Saint-Germain. But there was nothing mean or ill-lit about Charley's. It sported the only neon-sign in sight, and the bar itself, bathed in a bluish twilight, was done in false pickled oak. The bottles on the shelves were lit from behind, a whole keyboard of softly glowing colours that invited you to test out the barman's technique by ordering some strange, potent elixir.

I ordered two gin-and-tonics, more to test the barman's Englishness than his drink-making technique, though one look at that filleted nose, at that raw face seamed with white, was almost as good as a formal introduction.

"I don't often get asked for gin-and-tonic—especially in winter—would you like a spot more ice in it, Miss?"

I said: "French barmen don't usually know the drink. But you're English, aren't you?"

He shrugged his shoulders like a Frenchman: "I'm from London. But I've lived here ever since the war and I've a French wife and kids—you want to see them?" He took out a wallet and handed us a snapshot of himself, stripped to the muscles and grinning toothlessly. One arm was round the neck of a pretty brunette and the other round two very photogenic children.

I said: "That picture seems to ring a bell . . . you're not by any chance *the* Charley who held the welter-weight title in the twenties and lost it to Pugnier in 1926?"

"The same. I never went into the ring again. Brains was all I ever had, and I nearly lost 'em in that fight. It was the wife who made me throw in the sponge, and I'm not sorry—I was getting slow for my weight. The doctors said I couldn't take much more."

"So you invested your money in this bar? I must say, it looks as if it proved a good investment."

"I can't complain. When I bought the place it was just a *bistro*, but you've got to keep up with the times, you know, if you want to attract a good class of customer. I've had famous people in my bar—Ernest 'Emingway, the author; Belmonte, the matador; Carpentier—pretty well all the great names . . ."

We allowed ourselves to be duly impressed. Then I said casually: "Talking of celebrities, do you happen to remember a fellow called Twight?"

"Twight?"—I had heard the name echoed so often that evening, by people to whom it was nothing but an uncouth, mirth-provoking sound, that Charley's reaction was unmistakably positive.

But at that moment his attention was distracted. A thick, dark man had come in with two blonde girls. The blondes towered over him, but the little man, shining and scented in his camel-hair coat, invaded the bar with personality. Charley called out: "*Bonsoir, maître!*" and as he was moving down the bar to greet him he said quietly over his shoulder: "I don't recollect the name you mention. Of course I get all sorts and descriptions in here, but I only get to know the regulars."

It seemed that the newcomer was a regular who hadn't been in for some time. He leant over the bar and a diamond flashed as he poked Charley in the stomach. Then he felt Charley's biceps and shook his head amid sycophantic laughter from the blondes.

"*Tiens!*" he said. "He still defends himself, does our Charley, what?" His voice suggested that his vocal chords had been pickled in alcohol and his accent struck me as unfrench. "He may have forgotten how to use his fists, but he still defends himself with his knife and fork, what?"

Charley laughed without amusement. One of the girls leant over on her high stool and whispered into the little man's ear. He shook silently and slipped his arm round her waist so that his hand came up in front of her dress. "Give us a bottle of whiskey and three glasses."

As Charley set the bottle on the bar, the fat man said to him: "*Et la petite Jeannine?* How does she like you with a belly on you? Can you still defend yourself in love?"

Both girls laughed and the fat man, looking round for a larger audience, stared for a moment at Josephine, then tried to draw me into the conversation: "*Il faut se défendre dans l'amour, hein, monsieur?*"

I was rescued by a new arrival, a tall figure in a check cap and tweed coat, whom everybody hailed as 'Eddie'.

When they were all settled with drinks Charley came back to talk to us. "Noisy lot," he said, jerking his head in their direction, "but they're good customers. The fat one's a big fight promoter—a Corsican. Matter of fact he was once my manager. . . ." He made a quick gesture, extending his palm and rubbing his thumb and forefinger together to indicate graspingness.

"And the Englishman? He looks a sporting type too."

"Oh, that's Eddie Browne. He's a proper comedian. And class too. You mightn't think it, but he belongs to one of the finest families in Ireland. I'm not snobbish myself, but I know a gentleman when I see one."

"Perhaps that's why you didn't know Twight. He wasn't a gentleman, was he?"

We had been talking quite softly, but the others were making such a noise that I must have raised my voice to make sure Charley had got the name Twight. Silence fell on the bar. Charley looked curiously wooden and I knew they were all looking at me. As Josephine put it afterwards, it was as if a cracker had been dropped in a bucket of water.

I looked round and said loudly to Charley: "Well, whatever has passed over our graves, I'm very sure it's not an angel."

There was a neighing laugh from Eddie Browne and I heard him say in the execrable French of the true aristocrat: "*Pahlons pluto d'oatres shows.* As I was saying, *cher ami*, when you stopped listening to *my* conversation . . ."

Charley said: "I told you, I've never heard of the chap you mention. There are plenty bars round here you know."

I tore a leaf out of my notebook and wrote: '*J. T. Twight, journalist. Committed suicide in Paris, June 1929. Known to have frequented* this *bar.*'

Charley glanced at it and his expression became insolent. The others were talking in subdued voices and he caught Eddie's eye and winked. "Yes," he said more loudly, "yes, I remember him. The name slipped my memory because we used to call him *Gueule-de-Loup*—Snapdragon. Bad business that suicide. Bad for my business anyway, having police and journalists nosing around questioning my customers. By the way, what's your job—historian?"

The question was intended for the gallery and it did not fail to produce a titter.

"No," I said, "I'm a sanitary inspector. I thought you might be able to help me track down a bad smell!"

He said: "I'm a French citizen, I keep a respectable bar, and I told the police all I knew at the time. Now if you want to question me again you must show me that you're entitled to. Otherwise, Sir, I'm afraid I shall have to ask you to hop it!"

"All right," I said, "don't get worried. As a matter of fact I'm only a freelance writer, interested in Mr. Twight's life-story. All I want is your impression of him in his last days."

"Sorry, nothing doing. You can't sell the same article twice over."

"Okay," I said, "what do I owe you?" I tore off another sheet of paper and wrote: "I'm *not* a detective, *but if you don't want the police round again* you'll be wise to repeat all you know about Twight. What about a private rendezvous to-morrow morning?"

Charley retired behind the till and scribbled quickly on the back of my paper. He passed it back to me with the change.

As we left I heard Eddie saying: "Now, Charley! No betting slips or you'll get your licence taken away!"

It was refreshing out in the chill of the street after the atmosphere in Charley's bar. When we reached the Boulevard Raspail Josephine said: "Let's go and sit in a café for a while." She was looking very tired and I told her so. But she opened her eyes wide and fluttered her eyelids at me, and that settled the argument.

We went into the first café we came across—one of those

vast crowded places, all bright lights and plush seats, where one is at home as one can never be in cosy little bars like Charley's.

"This feels better," I said, taking out Charley's note and studying it. "Well now, what did you make of Charley?"

"He didn't like us one bit, did he? But then nobody likes inquisitive people. It's hard on a popular girl like me going around with a sanitary inspector! Actually, I'm pretty sure he would have talked freely about Twight if those other customers hadn't been there."

I began: "Charley's an ugly-looking customer himself . . ."

Then I broke off. My scalp had gone tight, as it does at the Opera when the soprano hits the high note. "Look, Josephine. What do you make of this note of Charley's?"

It said: '*O.K., son. Brasserie de la Victoire, 26 rue de Rennes, 9 a.m.* But if I was you I'd keep my nose out of others bisness.'

"Well, I suppose one threat deserves another. But it's a step forward, isn't it? It means that he knows more than he told the police?"

"Yes, I agree. But the style, the writing? Doesn't that remind you of anything?"

She studied it again, leaning over the table with her head in her hands, scratching one ankle with the other shoe.

"Look out," I said, "don't set your hair on fire with your cigarette!"

She looked up, sucked at the cigarette and stared at me: her expression was veiled by the smoke curling up from her parted lips.

"That anonymous letter—the one in reply to your advertisement in *The Times*! Oh, Raymond, you mean Charley wrote it?" Her eyes shone.

"We'll check up. But I'm certain it's the same writing."

It was warm in the café, but we were already warmer than

I realized. We were discussing the best way of approaching Charley when Josephine said quietly: "Don't look round until I tell you to. But isn't the man sitting two tables away behind your left shoulder the Englishman we saw at Charley's?"

I took a quick look. "Yes, that's him, but he may be just pub-crawling like us. Anyway, we'll soon see. . . ." I signed to the waiter.

As we went out of the door I looked back. He was making for another door higher up the street, but as we passed that door there was no sign of him. We began to think it was a false alarm.

On the steps of the hotel we paused again to look back. This time there was no doubt about it. There he was, standing in the boulevard at the end of our street, ostentatiously studying an advertisement on a kiosk.

Josephine's room looked out on to the street, so I went up with her. As we climbed the stairs—the lift, of course, was out of order—I could see the night porter looking up at us. It must have amused him, after the registration incident, to see me going past my own room.

As Josephine was opening her door I said: "Don't switch on the light for a moment—I want to have a peep out into the street." The heavy velvet curtains were drawn and I had to fumble for a second to find the cord. While I was doing it Josephine came up close to me in the darkness. I felt her hair brush my cheek and I put my arm round her and drew her closer. Then I pulled the cord and opened the window. I was just in time to see Eddie Browne walk slowly past. A street lamp caught his brown polished shoes, and I could see the tweed cap swivelling as he read the name of the hotel.

"Okay," I said, "you can switch on. He's got our address."

"So what?" Josephine stood by the door looking puzzled and (I persuaded myself) a little frightened.

I shrugged my shoulders and said nothing. I watched her go over to the mirror and comb her hair. I was fascinated by her reflection, because at that moment I was thinking I would like to marry her, that it wasn't hopeless after all.

"So what?" she repeated, turning round to smile at me. There was a little curl on the side of her head that refused to go into place.

"So a lot of things. I want you to ring up your step-uncle and say you're coming to use that spare bed he always has ready for you. If these people take the trouble to follow us they've got something on their conscience. They're going to try and find out what we're up to, and if they don't like it. . . . Oh for God's sake, Josephine, this isn't funny!"

"I know it isn't, but you are!" She came over and sat on the bed beside me. Then without warning she threw her arms round my neck and kissed me.

"That's what's so sweet about you, Raymond. You know I'm tough, but you will treat me like egg-shell porcelain, you won't admit that any girl you approve of has any right to be able to look after herself."

I started to protest, but she kissed me again, and this time I wasn't reluctant. I lay beside her, propped on my elbow, tracing the little smile-brackets round her mouth and running my fingers through her hair while she looked up at me thoughtfully and played with a button on my sleeve. It was strange to be so close to her, so close that her eyes had no depth or expression, only surface and texture like green enamel. I was glad I didn't know what she was thinking, because I was sure, in my unconquerable diffidence, that so far as she was concerned this was only a further stage in her attempt to explore the unfamiliar, exasperatingly remote maleness that Millington-Forsett had put in her way.

"And last night?" I said. "Was it last night or the night

before, when you found out I liked Stevenson?—who were you really thinking of?"

"Oh, I was just exasperated: you shouldn't take me seriously. The men I respect are always detestable, and yet I wouldn't have them otherwise."

I said: "But I did take you seriously. Come on, it's important now, and you promised to tell me. . . ."

He was an explorer-anthropologist. She had fallen for him when she was seventeen and he was twenty-eight, hero of two adventures in the jungle. He didn't discover that he loved her until shortly before his departure from England on a scientific expedition to the upper reaches of the Amazon, and by that time his heart was so engrossed in his project that the prospect of being separated from Josephine didn't worry him unduly: he was content to think of marriage at the end of a perspective that was all the more alluring for being long.

He disappeared into the Interior, and the flow of letters dwindled. For months she had no news whatsoever. And then she heard that the expedition was returning without him: he had been drowned navigating some rapids. . . .

Her parents flung her into a London Season and she went through it like an automaton—dance after dance, party after party, taking part in a parade of silly girls who were 'darling' to one another when they were together and 'that bitch' when they were not. Young men drove her about in fast sports cars and everybody drank too much: lovemaking stopped just short of disaster. Several young men wanted to marry her and she led them on ruthlessly until they came up against the void where her heart had been. It was partly the frustration of being unable to do more than *compete* in that narrow exclusive marriage-market that finally pushed her into an engagement. He was attractive, of good family, and skilful with women; and when it dawned on her that she didn't love him at all, but had been merely warmed and excited into a kind of euphoria, she revolted against the life she had been leading, and after a short period in Paris, went to work in Hodge and Ricketts.

She began to educate herself fiercely, schooled by the Hodge and Ricketts circle of intellectuals, with Hodge as her chief mentor. One of that circle, a Welsh poet with real bardic fire and a taste for drink, fell desperately in love with her, and for a time she was entranced to find her heart responding to his passionate verbal wooing. But gradually she came to see the weak, unstable creature who owned the bardic fire and after a series of appalling scenes she broke with him. He left her nothing but a bad reputation for heartlessness, and the feeling that she was incapable of ever falling in love again. . . .

It was at this point that I came in, a more mature and solid version of the pipe-smoking young man in the open-necked shirt whose photograph appeared over the brief biography on the dust-cover of *A Twist Somewhere*.

"You see," she said, "I just couldn't get away from you. Do you remember when you came into the office and found me climbing over those piles of books, all by you, all in the way? Do you know, there are moments when you remind me so strongly of those books that I want to take a duster and do you all over!"

I laughed formally. She was free with her kisses all right, but I had a strong feeling that she had not been so generous with herself. I got up from the bed and sat in the armchair.

"What was it the explorer did to you?" I asked.

She lay looking up at the ceiling and I thought she wasn't going to answer. Then she said: "He didn't know—how could

he have known?—that it would have been better to have
seduced me completely than to leave me with the unimportant
half of my virginity. His sort of love was a mixture of high-
minded sensuality and emotional neglect—he didn't think
those things really mattered—and I didn't think so myself
till afterwards. Then I found that my heart and my body had
quite separate ideas. . . ."

As we were saying goodnight I said: "So that's fixed,
isn't it? You'll go to your uncle's in the morning?"

I felt her stiffen in my arms and draw away. "So I've got
to sit making conversation to my step-uncle while you're
having fun and games in the Paris underworld? I might as
well go back to London."

I said: "Most of the time we can be together. But I shan't
feel happy till you're out of this hotel."

"Or free either?"

"In a sense, no. Tomorrow morning, for instance. If I
meet Charley alone he might give me what I want: he certainly
won't talk to two of us."

CHAPTER EIGHT

Some Suicides Don't Like Heights

IT WAS OBVIOUS why Charley had chosen the Brasserie de la Victoire. It was a gloomy old-fashioned place with wooden partitions between the tables, and at nine o'clock it was still deserted except for the charwoman mopping the floor with chlorine-water and a couple of waiters unstacking marble tables. The bar was in the centre and I toured right round it, looking into the wooden loose-boxes, before I finally found him in the far corner. Even then I had to look twice. Clad in a thick blue sports-sweater with a white line across the chest and arms, dunking *croissants* in a big bowl of *café-au-lait*, he looked more French than the French, and very different from the white-coated *patron* of Charley's Bar. He looked older, too, and his face was ashy with grey stubble.

As my shadow fell across him he looked up quickly from the sporting page of his morning newspaper and said: "*Salut!*"

"Good morning, Charley. I'm glad you've chosen a nice quiet place." I sat down opposite him, then remembered to get up again and peer ostentatiously round the corner of the partition.

"I just wanted to make sure nobody followed me in here!"

"What's the matter, eh?"—Charley was picking his teeth, and he spoke out of the corner of his mouth—"you've been reading too many tec-stories, Mister!"

I said: "You should read some too—you'd recognize the types in your bar. Last night I had one of them following me round all the evening—the aristocratic one, Eddie Browne. He wanted to find out where I was staying, I suppose."

In the pause that followed Charley asserted himself by

banging his coffee-cup with his spoon. When nobody came he shouted: "*On se fout des clients ce matin, hein?*" explaining, "in this country you've got to look after yourself or they take you for an imbecile."

He seemed nervous and impatient, so I made no comment and started filling my pipe in the slow deliberate way that infuriates even my best friends. He lit a *Gauloise* and glanced at his watch. Then he said: "Suppose you tell me why you want to dig up Mr. Twight?"

After I had wasted four matches lighting my pipe, the waiter came to take my order. By the time Charley got his answer his nerves were tuned to concert pitch.

"I want to dig up Twight because he was murdered, and it's only fair to tell you that at the moment you're the only link between him and his probable murderer."

He stared at me with cloudy blue eyes that seemed to swell uncomfortably in their raw-looking sockets. When he found his voice it was shadowy. "I don't know what you're on about. As far as I'm concerned Twight drowned himself. He was an alcoholic and he was broke: and when his girl put him against the ropes he just couldn't take any more punishment. As far as I know, nobody cared whether he lived or died."

"What about Millington-Forsett? Didn't he want Twight out of the way?"

Charley looked puzzled: "You mean the bloke that sued Twight for libel? Of course he didn't like him. But he got his money, didn't he? Why should he want to murder him too?"

He leant forward and tapped me on the sleeve: "Look, Mister, maybe you've got hold of something: I don't say you haven't. But you've got hold of the wrong end of it, see? I don't know nothing about this gentleman except what I've read in the papers."

"Well then, how do you explain this note, written recently in response to an enquiry about him in the Personal column of *The Times*?"

As I took the note out of my wallet, he cocked his head on one side, like a dog listening to a rat in the woodpile. I read four words of it and then he made a snatch: "Give me that paper and I'll stuff it down 'is . . . throat!"

I handed it over, enquiring mildly: "Whose throat?"

"Never you mind. But I'll tell you this much, it's the truth I don't know Millington-Forsett. One night in the bar a customer comes up and says: 'Charley, there's a compatriot of yours annoying me and I've written this note to warn him off. If you'll just put it into English for me, I'll copy it out and send it off!' . . . And that's all there was to it. He must have sent it off just as it was. If you don't believe me . . ."

"I do believe you. But I must know who this Frenchman was. He didn't care if he got *you* into trouble, did he?"

"Sorry, mate, there's nothing doing."

"Then either you're involved in this business yourself, or you know the people that are and you're frightened of reprisals."

He thought for a moment. "Suppose I just don't want to talk—I'd like to know what you think you can do about it?"

While I was trying to persuade him that I was *somebody*, and that the police of two countries would soon be on his tracks, he was running his hand over his grey, stubbly face as though trying to reassure himself that he really was Charley and not some frightful criminal. Then I remembered the family photograph he had shown with such pride: "And what about your wife and kids. Do you want them mixed up in this too?"

That did it. He suddenly looked miserable.

I went on persuading him for some time. Finally he said: "All right, Sir, but you're asking me to take a big risk. If Mattei finds out I've talked to you . . ." He clicked his fingers so loudly that I started, and a waiter, hovering not far away, came hurrying to find out if we wanted anything.

"Who's Mattei?"

"The fat bloke you saw in the bar. It was him set me up in business after I'd lost my ring-savings in a bookmaking concern. He lent me the dough and brought me the custom, and the only string attached to it was that I kept my mouth shut about everything that went on in the bar. . . ."

"And what did go on in the bar?"

"It was the centre of a prostitution racket." Charley fished under his sweater and brought out a well-thumbed *Guide to Paris Nightlife*. Under 'Bars and Cabarets' I read: *Charley's. International Atmosphere. Personalities from all countries rub shoulders with leaders of the Sporting and Intellectual world.* He could not conceal a certain pride as he added: "But it was high-class prostitution. Some of the girls was ladies and they all spoke more than one lingo. Of course there was respectable folk came to the bar too. It's right that Ernest 'Emingway and . . ."

"So it was Mattei who wrote the letter?" I cut in firmly.

Charley seemed amused by that suggestion: "The geezer who brought it to me was a little *garçon-de-café* I used to play billiards with in the old days—they call him Le Jockey in the *milieu*. . . ."

"Was there any connection between Mattei and Twight? Any business connection, I mean?"

"Not direct, that I know of. But if you ask me, Twight's girl was working for Mattei. Attractive piece she was, like vanilla ice with hot chocolate sauce—and a proper little actress too. With some geezers it was *chéri* this and *chéri* that.

But with Twight she was real ladylike—I used to laugh sometimes, despite myself."

"And *Gueule-de-Loup* fell for all this?"

"He seemed sweet on her all right—at the time. But then I found out something that didn't add up. *On the night he was drowned he had a date with a girl*"—Charley paused dramatically, his head thrust out of his high-necked sweater like a turtle in a confidential mood—"*and not the tart he'd been going round with neither!* From what I overheard one night in the bar—and I've never spoken of it to a living soul—this tart was the real goods. She worked mostly on the Normandy coast and Mattei's boys called her *La Futée . . .*"

"*La Futée?* What on earth does that mean?"

" 'A deep one'—'a dark horse', you might say. Most of these tarts have nicknames, especially if they're in some racket."

"H'm. . . . That certainly doesn't add up. And now I come to think of it, what was Mattei doing, letting these high-class prostitutes spend their precious time on a broken-down journalist? It certainly wasn't philanthropy!"

"That's for you to decide, Sir. But I wouldn't call him 'broken-down'—not until the end anyway. When he first came to my place he was flush with money. Later I reckon he wasn't so flush. But he kept spending just the same, because he was expecting money any day. And big money too. One night, when he was in my place with the dark tart, he was on about taking her to the Riviera. 'When my horse comes home . . .' he kept saying. But if that horse ever did come home, I reckon by that time it must have changed owners!"

I was too excited to be thorough. I had a feeling of weeds growing under my feet.

"Charley," I said, "what happened last night after we left the bar? Were there any questions asked?"

"Well, Eddie Browne did enquire about you casual like. But when I told him my lips were sealed he just laughed and said: 'Charley, I love you—you'll go far, like Mr. Baldwin!'"

"And Mattei? Did he have anything to say?"

"He said something to Eddie I didn't get, and shortly afterwards, when Eddie went out, he says to me: 'Eddie's a terror for the skirts. Did you see how he went after that English piece?'"

The end of this talk with Charley haunted me like the smell of burning rubber in the cold clear winter air. I hurried back towards the hotel far more worried about Josephine than elated by all Charley had told me.

I was pondering Mattei's remarks about Eddie and had just thought of a most unpleasant explanation, when the image of Eddie, as I had last seen him sauntering under our bedroom window, was suddenly shattered into a thousand pieces. He was coming towards me in a direct line. He had a Cairn terrier on a lead. Hatless this time and without an overcoat, his shoulders were shrugged, and his hands, thrust deeply into his pockets, wrapped his jacket tightly round his hips, so that with his drain-pipe flannels and his rather swooping walk he reminded me of a tweed kite being pulled gently along the pavement.

I looked away quickly, but he had already seen me.

"Hullo," he said in his cultured voice, which was pitched just too high to be pleasant, "haven't we met before somewhere?"

I continued to walk and Eddie fell into step beside me. "Damn cold, isn't it? You don't mind if I tag along for a bit? Actually it's rather luck my bumping into you: I happened to hear you talking rather loudly last night about a man I used to know, and though it was none of my business of course, I couldn't help pricking up my ears. You see, I used to be engaged to a cousin of John Twight's—lovely girl called Stella"—he removed a hand from his pocket and sketched copious curves in the air—"so I thought since you were a friend of his you might possibly have some news of her?"

I was rather disconcerted by this approach, but I thought I knew how to handle him. "You mean Stella Fanshawe—the dancer at the Palladium who married a chap in the Scots Guards?"

"Why, yes"—he looked at me blankly—"how is the little circus pony?"

"As a matter of fact she died some years ago. But before she died she asked me to come to Paris one day and say a prayer over John's grave!"

Eddie said: "Good God! I never heard! I say, we ought to get together, you know. Couldn't we have a spot of luncheon?"

"All right. But first I must just nip into my hotel and tell my girl I won't be able to 'luncheon' with her—otherwise she'll think I've fallen among thieves!"

Eddie neighed appreciatively. "I say, couldn't you bring her along too? Bit dull, with just the two of us."

I left Eddie standing on the pavement outside the hotel and went straight to the reception desk, where there was a message from Josephine telling me to ring her at her step-uncle's. I went up to my bedroom to do it and she answered the telephone in person.

"*Darling*," she said, "I've been sitting over the phone ever since I got here—I was beginning to panic. Are you coming round here straight away or shall we meet out somewhere for lunch?"

I said: "I can't. I've just run across an old friend and I've got something important to discuss with him."

"Who is he?" Her tone was chilled. "Why can't I come too?"

"Because he's asked *me* to lunch. I'll tell you all about him tonight. Shall I come and collect you about six?"

"Oh, just come along when you've run out of more important engagements. Yes, all right, six. My step-uncle wants us to have a drink with him. He's . . . Oh, there he is coming in! Goodbye . . ."

"Oh, Josephine?"

"Yes?"

"I don't want to fuss, but take care of yourself. If you must go out this afternoon, repeat *must*, keep on the Right Bank and take taxis . . . and, Josephine? . . . Hullo? . . ."

But she had rung off.

I found Eddie in the hall, sitting in an armchair smiling blandly.

"Lucky devil to have a girl like that," he sneered. "I hope you won't be offended if I suggest she must be finding it very dull in Paris, staying in her bedroom all day. None of my bloody business of course."

I said: "To tell you the truth she's not very well today. Anyway, I don't think she'd enjoy herself much listening to our reminiscences of Stella Fanshawe. By the way, my name's Kennington."

"Mine's Browne—Eddie Browne. I'm one of the original Irish Brownes, but I'm the Black Sheep of the family, so if you ever meet any of my relatives, you'll be wise not to mention me."

We lunched at a little Russian restaurant just round the corner from my hotel.

"It's like hell's kitchen," said Eddie as we entered. "But

there's always plenty of *crayme frayche* (that's sour cream, in case you don't know French) to keep the fire-water off the lining of your stomach. And don't be put off by the waitresses. They may look strait-laced, but they're all grand-duchesses really and they can't afford to be as grim as they'd like to be. . . . *Bonzure*, Olga!"—he chucked a middle-aged waitress under the chin—"*vous ate toozure ohsee bell!*"

He had challenged me to lunch with him. Now he challenged me to a flask of Doubrovka: "Well, *Dos Vidanja!* And down with Hitler and the Reds! . . . Now what are you really after? . . . I mean, was Stella really so cut up because her cousin died in mortal sin?"

"No, that's just the point. She thought it might have been an *accident.*"

"Accident? But my dear old boy, didn't she read the newspapers? Didn't she read the letter he wrote to his girl?"

"She did. But her feminine instinct refused, in the teeth of all the evidence, to believe that our friend John was the type to despair. And frankly, nor do I."

"Ah, there I can't agree with you. He was visibly breaking up, even before that girl gave him the push. Never sober for a moment. You remember how dreadfully his hand always shook?"

"I certainly do."

"And that rolling movement with his shoulders, as though his braces were too tight? . . . You do? . . . Well, you can imagine how his morale had sunk by the end . . ."

A tiny high-light of amusement in Eddie's eye, together with the intonation of 'you do?' gave me a sensation of mercury falling in my spinal column. I had been one up: now we were quits. I had called his bluff about Stella Fanshawe: but he now knew I had never known Twight! But all he said was: "Have some more Doubrovka, old boy? If we had ever met before, this would be quite like old times!"

The vodka glasses were genuine ones. They made the liquor seem to dwindle towards a vanishing-point at the bottom almost as soon as one had taken the first sip. My slip made me reckless instead of cautious. I gulped and said:

"All the same, that suicide doesn't convince me. Surely he wouldn't have gone all that way out of Paris just to throw himself in a nice quiet bit of the Seine. What's wrong with the Pont Neuf?"

"Some suicides don't like heights," said Eddie. "As a matter of fact they generally cover quite a lot of ground looking for the right spot. If you don't feel right, you can't bring yourself to do it, as I know from my own experience when Stella jilted me for that Cold Cream guardee. I was in too great a hurry to fade from the world and I muffed my exit completely. My last dinner on earth came up in the gasoven, and that quite put me off dying! . . . But seriously, old man, apart from your intimate knowledge of John Twight and your loyalty to our mutual flame, is there anything particular that makes you doubt the evidence of suicide?"

I was still sober enough to go through the motions of thinking; already drunk enough to try a long shot in the dark.

"Yes, there is one thing. I happen to know that at the time of his death he was expecting big money—and from a source that you'd never guess. From none other than Claude Nevil Millington-Forsett!"

Eddie was drinking at that moment and he did the nose-trick with Doubrovka, spluttering it all over his yellow cardigan.

"So that's why you're interested in Twight! Now that explains everything. Far be it from me to try and put you off —but aren't you casting your net in rather dangerous waters?

I mean, if I were you I wouldn't go about telling people that.
You remember what happened to poor John?"

"Oh, I'm not afraid of libel, if that's what you mean. And
if you mean—to coin a phrase—*that I might get the push
too?* . . ."

Eddie looked at me admiringly. He shook his head and
stroked the corner of his mouth.

"Terrific!" he said. "Extraordinary imagination! I say,
where can I get hold of your books?"

Eddie was presumably a Doubrovka addict. The stuff
seemed to have no visible effect on him and he must have
been noting my responses stage by stage. The first sip had
made me feel as though my tonsils were in the grip of surgical
forceps under an inadequate local anaesthetic. The second,
much bigger, seemed definitely tolerable—the anaesthesia
was working and there was a pleasant sensation of the gullet
being caressed. Thereafter, as glass succeeded glass, I felt
like a trout being tickled. I felt streamlined and invulnerable,
unconscious of the shadow hovering on the strong waters.
Eddie was there, an enemy who was out to catch me: yet
Doubrovka was also there, the ally in whose benign potency
I floated trustingly. . . .

The real split in my personality occurred without warning.
I had never been able to stand much teasing and the alcohol
had sapped my sense of proportion.

"Browne," I said, "you think I'm just a fool, don't you?
Well, let me tell you, *ole boy*, that I know a helluva lot about
thish Twight bishnish. I'm a famous writer with a public
what will tear you to bitch if you try to stop me getting the
truth. All blurry black sheep going to the slaughter, Claude,
Johnny and Eddie . . ."

I guess at my actual words from a clear memory of Eddie's
face, as he said: "But I want to help you . . . excuse me a

moment—I've just remembered I have to go and telephone."
I remember him getting up abruptly, being fascinated, first by
the leather pads on the elbows of his jacket, then by the way
his right pocket sagged with the weight of some heavy
object. . .

CHAPTER NINE

Progress in the Techniques of Love

I EMERGED from the Doubrovka about five o'clock. I was lying on my bed in the hotel surrounded by mauve parrots —hundreds of them, all exactly similar, pecking at bunches of bile-green grapes. I closed my aching eyes only to find worse than wallpaper within. On the shivering, silent optic screen the final scenes of my lunch with Eddie were being remorselessly projected. I could see myself following him to the telephone in the hope of overhearing some incriminating phrase—only to find him teasing a girl about her performance in some nude revue. I could see myself glancing nervously at his bulging pocket every time he put his hand into it, and I relived every second of my embarrassment when Eddie, becoming aware of my curiosity, and perhaps guessing what was on my mind, brought out the snowstorm paperweight he had bought that morning in the Rue Bonaparte.

Despite the aspirin and water treatment, I felt like a ghost gliding up the stairs to Stephen Wildbore's flat in the Rue D'Alger.

According to Josephine, her mother had married his brother Cecil because life with her first husband, Canning, had been so stimulating that she couldn't help falling for a name like Wildbore.

He was waiting for me at the top of the stairs, a handsome man in his middle forties who had only to smile and say 'hullo' for me to feel that stagey, bulb-and-canvas warmth which, in social professionals, comes on automatically. He was dressed impeccably in what I have always thought of as a Savile Row suit, with that careful touch of nature, the woolly cardigan, which says 'don't take the uniform seriously'.

"How nice of you to come," he said. "I'm afraid Jo isn't back yet. She's been out since nine o'clock this morning, but I'm expecting her any minute now."

I suppose my face must have turned slightly green—it couldn't have gone any whiter: for he added quickly: "It's just like her to be late."

I said: "I advised her to stay in. I hope she's all right?"

"Of course she's all right. She rang up ten minutes ago to say she had run into a friend and would be a bit late. Now what can I offer you—some whiskey or a Dry Martini?"

"Whiskey," I whispered, "and not too long. She didn't say who this friend was, did she?"

He looked at me rather queerly. "No, she didn't." Then added, with what struck me at the time as pure ghoulishness: "But if you're worried about the White Slave Traffic, I can promise you that young woman knows how to look after herself. She's knocked about quite a bit. . . . Well, here's to you and Jo, and to the success of your Millington-Forsett book!"

As we chattered on about Josephine, I had the impression that he was trying to put me at my ease, to show how broad-minded he was about this, the latest of her little fugues in Paris. It soon became obvious that Josephine, for reasons I couldn't guess, had been playing up the romantic side of our relationship at the expense of the detective side.

I was doing my best to correct this impression, telling him about my interview with Charley, and how that alone had made my trip to Paris worth while, when Wildbore quietly interrupted me:

"There she is at last, *la petite futée*!"

"Sorry I'm late," said Josephine unrepentantly, turning

sideways in the doorway to get through with all her parcels. "I simply had to have a drink with Hugh Anstruther, because the poor wretch had been carrying all my parcels for me. I do hope you two haven't been boring each other. . . . Well, what do you think of my hair?" She looked from Wildbore to me and back to Wildbore. "It really won't look like anything till I've combed it out."

"Frightful," I said, thinking more of the odd affectation in her voice, "I can't think why girls with soft, straight hair must go and have hard curls put in it. One needs to see you in a mirror not to be turned to stone!"

Wildbore said: "Oh come, Kennington, she looks ravishing. No wonder English girls give up trying!"

It was true. She did look ravishing, but like thousands of other pretty girls who allow hairdressers and dressmakers to model them from a glance at the exterior. It was a shock to me, just as I thought I was getting to know her. What was worse, she looked exactly as I imagined Hugh Anstruther, judging from her description of him, would have wanted her to look.

Hugh was the man she had been engaged to.

I could hardly bring myself to speak to her until I had got her alone in a restaurant. Then I said: "What's happened to you, Josephine? You've changed, and I'm not thinking only of your appearance. What about Hugh?—you didn't just 'run into him', did you?"

"Well? You can lunch with your friends. Why shouldn't I have drinks with mine? You ought to be glad I had an escort. Actually I was lonely, and I happened to know Hugh was in Paris."

"I was lunching with Eddie Browne, but I didn't want to tell you because I thought you might have been worried."

"Worried? I should have been furious! Do you expect me to sit at home all day like a medieval bride while you're performing feats of derring-do? If you didn't want me in Paris, why didn't you stop me coming?"

"So last night meant nothing whatever to you?"

"Last night?" She looked puzzled.

"Yes, have you completely forgotten?"

"My dear, what was there to forget! You were very sweet and protective, and nicer than I've ever known you be. You dragged my life-story out of me, then tore yourself away to plan today's campaign."

"Did I really behave so badly?"

"You behaved beautifully, that was the trouble."

"But, Josephine, we had all this out last night and the night before—must we go back over the agreement every night?"

"It looks like it, doesn't it? I do the agreeing. I just smile and sign and it's all settled, all *reasonable* and satisfactory! . . ." Her skin was very fair, and as she checked herself, I noticed an ominous flush round the cheekbones and under the eyes.

She stubbed out her cigarette furiously.

"What's the use of going on like this? I'm tired of being reasonable. I'm tired of chasing after you, yapping, and you not bothering to turn and look at me. That's why I got in touch with Hugh today. He wants me—and he does it without making me feel like a whore. It was just like the bad old times—a holiday from this deadly Millington-Forsett affair, from your smugness and beautiful behaviour. Look at you now! You're too pleased with yourself to be jealous, even. You're just embarrassed at this unseemly outburst!"

The flare-up was so sudden that I was stunned into taking her seriously. It was bad enough to be criticized, at a moment when I needed all my self-confidence, for behaving as well as I knew how to behave. But when she spoke of the Millington-Forsett affair as 'deadly', I felt insulted as well as injured. That left absolutely nothing.

"As you will, Josephine," I said. "I just knew it wouldn't work. But now I know where we are, I'm going to get on with the job I came to do, and leave you to enjoy your holiday with Hugh—he's more your type than I am."

She caught the harsh overtone of this remark, and said quickly:

"But I don't happen to love him."

"You don't love anybody—you told me so yourself. But since he apparently loves you, he's presumably prepared to put up with your caprices . . . *and* your new personality. . . ."

Shortly afterwards I left her at Stephen Wildbore's. I was already regretting what I had said, but I would have lost too much precious face by making a gesture of reconciliation. She said goodnight in a small, flat voice, and I accepted this restful finality as permanent, though I knew perfectly well it could only be temporary.

The fact was, I had made a great stride that night in the technique of love. I, who had always despised coquetry in any form, found myself positively wallowing in this quarrel. I was happy to get away and sulk, to sit alone in a dim café trying to persuade myself that all was lost. It only needed an extra drink or two to bring on a detached agreeable anger, directed less against Josephine than against the whole monstrous regiment of women. . . .

Then I remembered Twight's girl.

I was half-way to the telephone cabin before the idea was even clear in my mind.

"Is that Charley? . . . This is Raymond Kennington. . . .

How can I get in touch with Twight's girl—the brunette he was supposed to have loved?"

"Try the Toison d'Or, Place Blanche. . . . Her name's Marcelline."

"And what does she look like? . . . I mean, are there any visible distinguishing features?"

Charley chuckled lewdly: "That depends. If by 'visible' you mean 'outstanding' . . ."

"No, I don't. Has she got a hare-lip, cross-eyes, a moustache or gold teeth?"

"Well, I don't know as I remember anything un*usual* . . . she speaks French with an English accent and English with a French one—you know, a bit la-di-da. But now she's come down a bit in the world she probably talks more like the *milieu*. . . . Wait a minute, though, there *was* something. . . . I think she has a beauty spot in the corner of one eye. . . ."

I plunged into the nearest Metro, to emerge half an hour later blinking in the glare of the Place Blanche. The cold made my eyes run and the water made the lights run together in great splashes of colour as I stood for a moment bewildered by the noises of the fair in the middle of the Square—the cries of the *forains*, the wheezy music of the roundabouts, and the rattle of the shooting-galleries.

"*Approchez, monsieur*," someone called, "*vous pouvez gagner une bouteille de champagne.*"

I turned round and saw a sad-eyed woman gazing at me from a booth. Encouraged, she said in English: "Okay, come on. For five francs you win champagne."

There was nobody else there, so I put down five francs and she pushed over five darts and a battered air-pistol with a plastic butt.

"I don't want your champagne," I said, as the first dart scored an outer. "I want to buy one of these pistols."

I think she thought I was drunk as well as mad. She began to look cunning.

"These pistols aren't for sale—they are made specially for us by a famous firm of gunmakers."

"Well, you'll have to get rid of this one soon—it doesn't shoot straight."

"*Tant pis!* That isn't the fault of the pistol, monsieur. All these pistols are tested regularly. But if you are accusing me of cheating you, here are your five francs back. *Allez, monsieur, amusez-vous ailleurs, nous sommes des gens sérieux.*"

I said: "If you're honest, let me borrow this pistol and test it for myself."

She blew out her cheeks and made a contemptuous noise. "My husband isn't here tonight or he would show you how to score ten successive bulls with that pistol—*m'enfin*, if you really want to borrow it, it will cost you six thousand francs. Five thousand back if you return it tomorrow."

I was in too much of a hurry to haggle. I put down the notes and she scribbled a receipt. I didn't even bother to turn back when she said: "*Tenez, je vous donne cinq dards.*" The pistol was in my pocket and I didn't need any darts.

It didn't take me long to find the Toison d'Or—a curious wig-like sign was transfixed by a golden arrow pointing down an alley. A man with a padded dinner-jacket relieved me of my coat and led me down a spiral staircase to a long barrel-vaulted room that reminded me of the vaults of the House of Commons all set for the gunpowder plot. The tables were placed on wine-barrels and the dim lighting was filtered through sacking.

The place was practically empty, but as I came in the *patron* clicked his fingers and the whole thing sprang to life like a peep-show when the penny drops. A saxophonist, a drummer and a pianist, doodling with the instruments on a raised plat-

form, began to play a tremulous Blues, and some tired-look-
ing girls sitting near the platform suddenly stopped yawning
and began to make up their faces, glancing at me from behind
their mirrors. It was enough to make anybody feel self-conscious, but the outsize air-pistol in my pocket imposed an
impressive swagger on my walk and I made for a table opposite the girls, whistling nonchalantly through my teeth.

"Monsieur is alone? You like to dance?"

"Later. First bring me some champagne."

While I was waiting I smoked and looked the girls over.
There were two brunettes, and I had just persuaded myself
that the fatter one was Marcelline, when the whole spider's
web was set vibrating by the arrival of two blond Scandi-
navians, who had been enticed, I gathered, by a tout from the
Moulin Rouge. They were very young, singing drunk and
wearing white student caps on the back of their heads. The
two potential Marcellines rose like one woman and went over
to join them without a second glance in my direction. I was
offended as well as perplexed. I called the *patron* over:

"Have you a girl called Marcelline?"

"*Mais oui.* You like to speak to her?"

"That depends. Will you point her out to me?"

"*Elle est là, au fond* . . . He pointed to a red-head sitting by
the stage, and seeing my face fall: "She is very nice lady,
sharming, *sympathique, intelligente.*"

"But does she speak English well? I want a girl I can talk
to."

He gave me a shopwalker's smile of perfect understanding
and bustled away clicking his fingers.

I was somewhat reassured by the refeened 'hullo' that
accompanied the limp, ladylike hand and the heavy onslaught
of tuberose. She had a full, voluptuous upper lip, badly let
down by a feeble jaw, so that her mouth disappeared into

shadows at the corners, forming a disappointed Giaconda smile. I couldn't see the beauty spot. But she was a brunette all right and she was certainly upholstered for her profession.

Under the plucked eyebrows, small restless brown eyes enquired how I knew her name. "I don't think I've seen you before. You must be a friend of Tommy? . . . of Joe then? . . . of Steven, no? . . . of Georges? Yes, I am sure you are a friend of Georges: he spoke very much about your work. . . ."

"No, none of these. I'll tell you later when we know each other better."

I poured out a glass of champagne and we clinked glasses. She said: "You come from London, don't you? Ah, I couldn't mistake. Now I will tell you more about yourself. You are gay, you like jokes, you seem to live on the surface. But underneath you are sad and full of *nostalgie*. You come to Paris to escape the fogs, the dark streets, the early closings: you have things to forget. . . ." Her voice was smokey, a parody of the Marlene Dietrich school of elocution.

"How well you understand me!" I sighed.

"But naturally! I am English myself—at least my mother was."

The mysterious smile suddenly extended up her face, so that I saw the beauty spot, a slight bump beneath the heavy makeup, caught between two converging wrinkles.

"Tonight we are gay," she was saying. "We drink champagne, we dance, we talk . . ."

"And then what?"

"Then we dance more and drink more champagne!"

"And then?"

"Then we go to bed."

"Together?"

"*Mais non, chéri.* You are serious like all the English boys. For you love is everything, the love-making nothing!"

"On the contrary," I said, forcing myself to move closer, "for me the love-making is everything!"

She wriggled coquettishly and said: "*Voyons, chéri,* you exaggerate!" Then she firmly grasped the champagne bottle and poured out two more glasses. "We pass the time *en bons camarades, hein?* We order more champagne, we have a good time."

"For God's sake!" I said. "You are beautiful and I want love. Can't we go somewhere else?"

"But, *chéri,* it is expensive to go somewhere else. You see, Victor is my *patron,* and if we go away others will ask for me and Victor will lose money. I tell you this because you are English and I like you very much. Victor likes too much money!"

"How much?" I said, with all the crudeness of my impatience.

"I will speak with him. But I don't think he will agree."

She soon returned, nodding and smiling mysteriously. I gathered she had known how to handle Victor.

She patted my cheek: "Now be a good boy and pay the bill while I'm getting my mantle. Victor says I mustn't be seen leaving with you—that wouldn't look quite nice."

The bill was exorbitant, of course, though Victor assured me he had made a special price because I had been introduced by a friend of Marcelline's.

"*Et à propos*"—he bent down and whispered in my ear— "if you want to go home with Marcelline, there will be a little *supplément* of five thousand francs . . . you are surprised? But, monsieur, this is a cabaret, not a *Maison de Tolérance.* These girls are all *artistes,* not public girls."

"Then why are you allowing her to come out with me?"

"To render a service, *comprenez-vous?* Marcelline explains

you are sad and she wants to make you 'appy. You are English gentleman, so you will not forget to give her a little *douceur* afterwards."

I said: "You put it very delicately. By the way, Victor, why is this place called the Golden Fleece?"

CHAPTER TEN

'To Marcelline with love from Johnny'

(1)

MARCELLINE WAS WAITING for me in a shadowy part of the passage and as we walked into the square I saw her for the first time in good light. The coppery sheen of her dyed hair and the blue shadows round her eyes gave her a kind of lurid poster attraction in the authentic Moulin Rouge tradition. But the promise her body communicated, as she took my arm and squeezed against me, did not extend above her clothes. There was no longer any mystery hovering about the corners of her mouth: the jaws met in a red curve, hard and definite as a pike's.

We turned into the Rue Caulaincourt, then up a steep cobbled street of cliff-tall impassive façades that seemed to lean together peering at their opposites. The dimness of the street-lamps under which we walked was emphasized by the reflected glare from the Boulevard Clichy striking the top storeys on one side of the street, and our crisp footsteps on the cobbles broke into the rhythms of accordeon music drifting down to us from some distant *bal musette*. When at last we stopped at Marcelline's the click of the door, opened by the hand of an invisible *concierge*, seemed to outrage the modesty of the whole street.

As I laboured after Marcelline up the iron steps of the spiral staircase, enormous shadows wheeled round the shaft, speeded by the ominous ticking of a light-saving device down in the basement. On each landing there were three doors painted the same public grey. Most had visiting cards pinned on them. But Marcelline's, on the third floor, was anonymous and without a number even. The light went off just as we reached it and for a moment as she fumbled for her latchkey I was imprisoned in the darkness with her heavy perfume sickeningly adulterated by the prevailing pungency of Eau de Javel and urine.

The room she illuminated was basically the typical furnished bed-sitter in the cheap parts of Paris: there was the big iron bed, the buff-coloured night table, the worn-out plush chair and the hanging place draped with a tulip-patterned curtain. There was the flimsy screen round the washbasin and the inevitable collapsible *bidet*. But it was the personal touches that caught my eye—the gas-fire with its glow of artificial coals, the Louis-Seize type dressing-table and the florid marble-topped table covered with photographs of men.

While she was lighting the gas-fire I went over to look at the photographs. It was a display of scalps, and judging by the inscriptions on them, practically all were of Englishmen. Twight—I was rather surprised to find—had a place of honour—Twight, wearing an old-school tie and an army moustache, looking as if butter wouldn't melt in his mouth. He had inscribed his picture 'To Marcelline with love from Johnny'. If I had been feeling sentimental this might have struck me as pathetic. As it was, I could imagine it had come in useful to build up the illusion of a shattered idyll.

"*Eh bien, chéri*, aren't you going to get ready?"

Marcelline had retired behind the screen; not, I am sure, for the sake of modesty, but because experience had taught her that her undressing would be more effective that way. She must have noticed that my ardour had cooled considerably between the cabaret and the bedroom.

"No. First I want to have a talk with you. The room hasn't warmed up enough yet."

"Silly boy," she said, "there's no need to be shy with Marcelline"—she added something I can't write down.

Presently she emerged, temptingly covered with a blue quilted dressing-gown, and knelt down in front of the fire facing me. She rested her head on my knee for a moment, expecting me to stroke her hair. When I didn't, she removed her head and looked at me hard.

"What a funny boy you are! *Dis, mon petit Raymond*, who was it sent you to me? Was it one of my boy-friends on the table over there?"

I hesitated, then I said: "Yes, Johnny Twight."

Her eyes hardened, but her mouth was still loose.

"Johnny was my best friend," I said.

She had tied her dressing-gown loosely at the waist so that the top gaped tantalizingly. At the mention of Twight she gave a slight shiver and drew the edges of her dressing-gown together so that her hands were crossed over her breasts in a gesture so instinctive that I felt the chill myself, the sudden lowering of the sexual and psychological temperature.

"But Johnny never spoke about you. He said all his English friends had deserted him."

"Never mind what he said. I didn't desert him and I've been waiting for years for this moment. I want you to tell me exactly what happened to Johnny. . . ."

"*Mais oui, chéri—je te dirai tout. Mais d'abord on va faire l'amour, hein?*" She was thinking so hard that she forgot to talk English, and when she saw the expression on my face she made a desperate effort to put me off. Her voice became husky with false desire as she said: "*Je te dirai tout si tu viens à moi.*" Then, with a swift and deliberate gesture she undid her dressing-gown and threw out her arms so that her naked body was exposed, quivering, from the throat to the knees. . . .

I looked at her for a moment, struggling with myself like John the Baptist in Oscar Wilde's *Salome*. Then I remembered what I had come for, and suddenly the plan I had evolved in the café became the only natural course of action. I became myself, the nursling of the nonconformist conscience, and the law and the prophets were on my side, not to mention Josephine.

I said: "Do yourself up and sit down in that chair," and when she moved closer to me, pressing her body against my knees, I slid the air-pistol from my pocket and, sitting back in my chair, pointed it at her without saying a word.

There was a bad moment when I thought she had recognized the pistol for what it was. As she hesitated I realized that it was now or never: I had to back the toy with words that sounded adult.

I said: "He loved you. He believed in you and you betrayed him. Now I've come to settle the account. So if you know how to pray, be quick about it. . . ."

I suppose women like Marcelline, dominated by dangerous men, are apt to take threatening males seriously. At any rate, I had caught her with her hair down, for her mouth sagged open and she put one hand up to her cheek, turning her head a little sideways so that she looked at me with eyes that were half white.

"No," she said, "no, no, no! He didn't love me. He *hated* me."

"That's a lie. He wrote you a letter on the night of his death. You owned up to the police and to the English journalist that you were the cause of his suicide."

"I only told he loved me because they made me. He wrote the letter just to be venged on me, because he was cynical and cruel."

"Who is 'they'?—do you mean Mattei's gang? . . . Come on, I want an answer quickly and I warn you, if you move or call out, I'll shoot—this is an airgun and the shot won't be heard beyond these walls."

She seemed to understand my language. Her eyes stopped wandering round the room and she relaxed. Then she got up and crouched down on the other side of the fire.

"Give me a cigarette."

With my free hand I tossed over my cigarette-case and some matches. She inhaled deeply, then she said:

"*Eh bien, tant pis.* You will shoot me if I don't tell. They will shoot me if I do!"

(2)

Her instructions, when she was 'introduced' to Twight, were to help him with his articles and to report about his contacts, though she never understood why. Then one day she got her marching orders again. She was told there was another job for her. A few days later she had a visit from one of the agents of the '*entreprise*', as the racket was called by those in it. Twight's body had been found in the Seine, she was informed. "And if the *flics* come along asking questions, just remember you were his only girl in Paris, that he loved you and you left him because of his drinking. That's your story, and if you don't stick to it, you may find yourself in the river too. Have you any gifts or letters to make the story convincing?"

That very morning she had received Twight's last letter.

"Why do you think they made you do that?" I asked.

She shrugged her shoulders listlessly.

"To cover some other woman, I suppose. Somebody more important to them than me."

"Did you ever hear of a girl called *La Futée?*"

She shook her head. "In the *entreprise* we girls only got to know each other by hazard. It was well organized—by men, you understand."

"And did they give you another job?"

"*Pensez-vous!* I wasn't any longer beautiful enough for

their rich clients. Besides I was known to the police. I was free to sell myself *au bon marché.*" She broke off and laughed bitterly. "Well, why do you stare at me? It's pretty, isn't it, the story of a prostitute?"

She was beginning to find relief in irony and self-dramatization and I felt I was losing the initiative. I said: "Yes, it's a very pretty story, all the prettier because you've invented most of it so as to throw the blame on somebody else. You did well out of Johnny, didn't you? And you thought you were going to do even better. But when you realized that the fortune he was expecting wasn't forthcoming, you left him of your own free will—drunken, desperate, and without a soul in the world but you. . . ."

She was licking her lips as though she had the taste of sloes on her tongue. She said quickly: "Did he tell you that his uncle in England had just died and that as soon as the testament was regulated he would be very rich? *Ça c'était déjà beau.* But he also promises that when he is rich he will marry me and together we shall go to *Amérique du Sud*! Of course I do not believe him. Why should he wish to marry me—why even trouble to make promises—when I am already his *maîtresse?*"

"Why indeed?" I echoed sternly. "Unless he was very fond of you."

"*Eh bien, oui!* sometimes I allowed myself to dream. That is why I was not *contente* when one evening—it was my birthday and he had promised to take me to a *chic* restaurant —I received a note that his *avocat* from England had arrived in Paris and that he was very sorry etcetera. *J'étais toute habillée*, ready to go out, and I did not believe this excuse. I went to his hotel and found that he had gone to take his bath. On the table in his room there was a typewriter and many sheets of paper. There was also a little note on the paper of the Hôtel Crillon: 'Meet me at eight o'clock Chez Maurice—

Milly.' I said '*Merde, ce n'est plus drôle, cette histoire!*' I ran out of the hotel and went to a little café just beside Chez Maurice. I stayed there a whole hour drinking *apéritifs* and then I went to Chez Maurice—*vous comprenez*, I was half drunk, I wanted to make a *scandale*—I was ready to tear the eyes out of this little *Anglaise*. . . ."

She leapt up as she said this and her nails ripped at the cloud of cigarette smoke she had just ejected. The gesture was pure Grand Guignol yet perfectly in accord with the unchained hatred in her voice.

She did not wait to be shown Twight's table. She swept into the restaurant and almost immediately spotted Twight. But by the time she had realized that his dinner companion was an old man and not a girl, it was already too late to turn back. Twight had been drinking heavily and as soon as he saw her his face flushed purple.

"What the bloody hell are you doing here?" he said, looking at Marcelline as though she were a bit of dirt instead of the girl he had promised to marry—"didn't you get my message that I was engaged tonight?" The old man intervened: "How do you do, my dear. Won't you sit down and join us?" The voice she remembered as soft and agreeable, and as the old man stood up courteously, she had the impression of distant, almost colourless eyes scrutinizing her through holes in parchment.

At first she thought he really was Twight's lawyer. Then he said something that made her look at him in a new way. He used a word that had puzzled Marcelline reading through newspaper clippings of Twight's libel action. 'I could do without the publicity,' Millington-Forsett had told an enterprising reporter, 'but I can't do without the *oof*.'

As soon as she realized who he was, she had an explanation for Twight's behaviour. He was obviously on tenterhooks lest she should find out the identity of his guest. He probably didn't trust her with his secret any further than he saw her. He was all the more worried because, for some reason she had never fathomed, Millington-Forsett seemed extremely anxious for her to stay, rallying her with old-world gallantries and asking all sorts of personal questions in the sly manner of old satyrs.

The following evening she dined with Twight. He surprised her by pretending that nothing had happened, and for her part she pretended that she had not recognized Millington-Forsett. To be more convincing she asked him if he had got the money from his lawyer.

"Not yet," he said grimly, "but if I don't get it in a week somebody's going to want a new lawyer."

After dinner they went up to Twight's room, and without any warning he turned on her and said: "So you read my private papers, do you? You want to find out everything so that you can blackmail me? All right then, here's some private papers you probably didn't have time to read last night."

It was ten pages of carbon-copy—notes for a pornographic novel about the life of a prostitute in Paris, containing a cruel description of Marcelline's face and physique, and an analysis of her character that stripped her bare with loathsome thoroughness. As she read on, determined to drink the bitterness to the last drop, she gathered that the episode of the promise had been nothing but a cold experiment to test her reactions. Mind and body, he had been using her as a model right from the beginning . . .

I said gently: "It's unspeakable, I can hardly believe it. Isn't it just possible that he wrote it in a cold fury *after* the Millington-Forsett episode, just to punish you for prying into his affairs. After all, he had reason to fear blackmail: he was a criminal."

"All men are criminals," she said, "there's a *solidarité* among men that the woman can never beat."

"And yet you still keep his photograph—why?"

"Because I loved him—he is the only man I ever loved."

She had begun to shake with dry convulsive sobs and I went over and put my arm round her shoulders. "I'm sorry," I said. "I swear I'll tell nobody what you have told me."

She looked up at me and said: "You are going already?"

She went over to the dressing table and gazed at her face. Then she started quickly dabbing powder on it. Without turning round she said in her old hard professional voice: "You are going to leave me without giving me a little present?"

I put down some notes and went to the door. Then I remembered the air-pistol I had left in the chair.

"Here you are," I said, "you can have this too—take it with this receipt to the woman at the shooting gallery nearest the Place Blanche Métro and you'll get five thousand francs for it."

I was standing on the pavement in the Rue Caulaincourt trying vainly to get a taxi when a voice said: "I say, old man, why don't you try the Place Clichy?"

I turned round quickly and there was Eddie with his dog. He had a copy of *The Times* under his arm.

"Don't look so startled," he said, "I won't tell your girl! I was just sitting in a bar at the corner and I saw you go past. I thought you looked rather stranded. Well, well, it's a small world, isn't it? Won't you come and have a nightcap?"

He looked down at his feet, whistling softly, as though he found the situation embarrassing. At the moment I saw a taxi and hailed it.

"Well, cheerio!" he called out as I drove away. "I expect I'll be seeing you sometime."

CHAPTER ELEVEN

La Futée

I HAD WORKED UP such nervous momentum, that when I eventually dozed off for a couple of hours, two trains of thought converged into an unpleasant dream. Josephine, *alias La Futée*, invited me to walk by the river. As we went she explained: 'It was horrible to have to keep pushing his head under every time he came up for air—it was worse than drowning a kitten.' I kept telling her she wasn't well.

I awoke with a strong feeling that I had to write down this dream, but by the time I was shaving I realized that what I wanted to do was to explore the place where Twight had been found. I had been persuaded while I slept that it was the only chance of finding some clue to the identity of *La Futée*.

By the time my train arrived at Corbeil the effect of this dream had completely worn off and I was beginning to regret the impulse. It seemed wildly improbable that ten years after the event in question I would find anything at all. But I told myself that I had planned to visit the spot anyway. I had a map of this part of the river and I thought I could easily get a bus to within walking distance of the lock where Twight's body had been found.

I had reckoned without its being Sunday. There was an hour to wait before the bus left, so I hailed a local tradesman's van which was going in the right direction.

He put me down at the nearest point on the main road to the stretch of river I was aiming at. There was a village, a grey, dilapidated place, apparently still fast asleep. It seemed to have no function whatsoever except to provide advertising space for Byrrh and Cinzano. But there was a *bar-tabac* and since I hadn't had anything to eat, I went in.

A faded woman with oily ringlets looked up from her *France-Dimanche*. A brave attempt to look welcoming ended in a yawn. But when I asked for coffee and *croissants* my accent seemed to arouse her curiosity.

"You are here for the weekend?" she suggested. "You are seeking tranquillity out of Paris?"

"Not exactly. . . . As a matter of fact I'm revisiting the place where I found romance when I was a young student at the Sorbonne. You remember the summer of 1929—how carefree life seemed? . . . But of course not. Madame must have been too young. . . ."

This time her smile succeeded. "Monsieur is gallant! How could I forget that year!"

It had been the year of her husband's death; and when she had exhausted his medical history, it was the easiest thing in the world to start her off again on the subject of the suicide at the barrage. She had been recently widowed at the time, and the lock-keeper's wife had come running to the bar, just when she was feeding the chickens. . . . It was strange, was it not, for a foreigner to drown himself so far from home?

"Very strange," I said, "but for me the strangest thing was that he drowned himself so far from Paris. I always wondered if it was really suicide."

"Ah, that's what Madame Moineau wondered too. She told me there was a mark on one of the ankles. *Mais que voulez-vous?* The pathologist who did the autopsy found nothing suspicious. And then afterwards, when the police found the letter and the girl, there was no longer any doubt. Madame Moineau was not convinced, however"—she gave me a long appreciative look, like an undertaker measuring a corpse for a coffin—"to think he was a compatriot of yours, and just about your age too!"

"I prefer not to. But about the mark on the ankle—what was it like?"

"Oh, just a bruise, some broken skin, as though he had caught his foot in something . . . *enfin, je ne sais pas très exactement.* You must ask Madame Moineau herself—she is never tired of talking about it." I was very thoughtful as I took the little road that led from the village to the towpath.

The lock-keeper's house was a white-washed building with faded blue shutters and a neglected look. Round the back of it I found a pretty girl of fifteen, peeling potatoes into a bucket. "Madame Moineau," she told me, "is at Mass. But if you want 'the lock-keeper', at this hour he'll be at Monsieur Castello's, drinking!"

"Monsieur Castello's?"

"The slipway, a kilometre from here. Just follow the towpath."

I followed the windings of the river along the wooded towpath, past houses half hidden in smoky winter copses, broken here and there by frosty fields lined with strict perspectives of poplar. All the traffic of the great river seemed to have dwindled to a single string of tarpaulin-covered barges, black and motionless at their warps, despite the energy of the current that spun and gurgled round their blunt noses.

Presently a bend in the river revealed the slipway. There was a cut in the bank, fenced off by a wooden pontoon to make a little haven for canoes and centreboard dinghies. A few derelicts lay warped and blistered on the concrete slipway. Rails disappeared under the sliding doors of a big shed.

As the place seemed shut up, I went round to the back, where I found a similar shed with a small side-door standing open. I could see nobody there either and when I called out, my own voice came back to me from the corrugated iron roof.

Inside I forgot what I had come for. There is a special fascination about boats laid up in the dead of winter, and I felt like a little boy in a shopful of giant toys.

I was edging between two sailing boats that towered over me, supported on wooden legs, when my eye caught the stern of a motorboat.

For a moment I just stared, unable to grasp the significance of the words painted upon it in letters of gold—

LA FUTÉE

DEAUVILLE

I reached up with both hands and putting my foot on the rudder stable hoisted myself up on to the deck. . . .

"*Qu'est-ce que vous faites là, monsieur?*"

The owner of the harsh voice was hidden by boats and there were some seconds of embarrassing hide-and-seek before I looked down on a bald head, mottled with brown alcoholic patches: the eyes, which were the colour of stale mustard, glared up at me angrily.

"*Descendez tout de suite.*"

I descended with as much dignity as possible in the circumstances.

"Who are *you?*" My moral position was so shaky that the only thing was to brazen it out. "I was looking for the *patron*, and since there seemed to be nobody about and the door of the shed was wide open I came in to have a look round. Now please take me to the *patron*."

My attitude impressed him more than my appearance. He looked me up and down critically, but spoke with a kind of sulky servility.

"I am the *patron*. What can I do for you?"

"So you are Mr. Castello—that changes everything." I advanced upon him with outstretched hand, and though he was still eyeing me (as they say) narrowly, he had no alternative but to take it. I hesitated, swallowed hard, then added: "I am from the British Embassy. We have heard that the owner of *La Futée* wishes to charter her next summer. My instructions are to see if the boat is suitable for the Counsellor and his family, who have taken a house on the river. . . ."

"I think you must have been misinformed. Monsieur Grosset telephoned only last week giving details of the new engine he wishes me to install this Spring. However, if you would like me to telephone? . . ."

"Monsieur *Grosset?* That's queer. I understood the owner's name was Mattei."

"Then there certainly is some mistake. Monsieur Mattei sold it years ago after it had been damaged by a mad Englishman with a mania for speeding on the river and spoiling this stretch for the sailing dinghies I hire out at weekends."

"But of course! That must be the man at the Embassy who told our Counsellor the boat was probably for charter. What was his name?"

"Braoun . . . Brouan . . . something like that. It is possible he was a diplomat."

"That's the man. In that case I think you had better say nothing till I've had another talk with him. Anyway I think the boat is rather small for the Counsellor and his family. . . ."

I handed him a thousand francs and he took it eagerly, looking at me with deep suspicion.

A yellow sky brooded over the return journey. In trains and buses passengers looked at one another curiously, discoloured like souls in the Underworld. But I was in high spirits, full of my good luck and determined to settle the absurd quarrel with Josephine.

I was coming along the passage outside my room when I heard my telephone ringing. I ran the rest of the way and pounced on the receiver, only to feel a shock of mingled disappointment and misgiving as I heard the voice that had been dogging me, patiently and cynically, for the last twenty-eight hours.

"Hullo, old boy. You sound rather out of breath."

"Well, Browne, what is it?" Surely he couldn't have already heard about my visit to the slipway?

"Well, actually, I'm having a drink with that delightful girl-friend of yours. She thought something might have happened to you, but since you're apparently alive and kicking, why don't you come round and celebrate?"

Desultory snowflakes were drifting past the window and I followed one down till it settled on the stone parapet of the balcony.

"How did you get her to have a drink with you?"

"I just rang her up and suggested us getting together."

"Think again. You don't even know her telephone number."

"Oh, but I do! You gave it me yourself when you rang her up from the hotel yesterday. I was sitting in the hall and I heard the porter repeating the number. But of course, if you don't believe she's here, I'll ask her to come and speak to you."

". . . Where are you?"

"5 Rue Renée Pauline, only ten minutes' walk from you. So long—Abyssinia!"

"I'll think it over. Goodbye."

I thought it over. Then I asked for Wildbore's number, and getting no reply, rang up the British Embassy, where the operator, reminding me that it was Sunday, advised to try the British Consulate. The Consul was out of Paris, but eventually I got through to a junior official who said that my worry sounded like one for the police, and that anyway he couldn't discuss the matter further unless I came round to see him . . .

I could have borne the anxiety and frustration more easily, if I hadn't had a strong suspicion that I was making a complete fool of myself.

I took a taxi to No. 5, Rue Renée Pauline, which turned out to be a bar. As I entered, Eddie cropped up from a table behind the door.

"Where's Miss Canning?" I demanded fiercely.

"Oh, she's in a flat just round the corner. I thought this place would be easier for you to find, so I've come along to fetch you, okay?"

I followed Eddie across the street and down an alley, one side of which towered suddenly and became the blank, blackened wall of a cinema. As we turned off it into a passage ending in a garage, I could see the tail of a cinema queue moving up the next street. An accordeonist, sitting on a stool with his back towards us, was playing the theme-song from *Sous les Toits de Paris*.

In the garage there was a long black Citroen being groomed by a chauffeur like a gorilla. Beyond was an office and Eddie led me through it, opening a door at the far end and standing back with mock ceremony: "After you, Claude!"

My first impression was that the room was full of faces staring at me. I suppose I had been expecting to fall into a trap. Actually there were only three faces—mine, Eddie's and Josephine's—reflected in a mirror on the wall opposite. She was sitting on a sofa hidden by the door and she gave me a gay, brassy smile, which didn't at all agree with the look in her eyes.

"Hullo, Josephine. Nice of you to ask me to join the party!"

"I didn't, but I'm very very glad you're here. I was just leaving for the boat-train when somebody telephoned to say that you had had an accident. By the time I found out you were safe, I had been kidnapped . . . oh, in the nicest possible way: I shall dine out on this story for weeks! Mr. Browne is a romantic. He was afraid you and I had quarrelled and he wanted to bring us together again before we left Paris!"

"Well, if that's all, it only remains to thank him. Come on!"

"*I'm afraid he's going to insist on our staying.*"

I turned round quickly. Eddie had a small black automatic in his hand.

"Sit down, Kennington, we've got to have a talk." He kicked the door shut so that the strains of *Sous les Toits de Paris* were cut off in the middle of a phrase. Then he swung his leg over the arm of a chair: the hand that held the gun dangled elegantly from the wrist resting on his knee.

"Please do as he tells you, Raymond." Josephine's appeal made me suddenly conscious of cutting a figure, and I remained obstinately standing.

"Browne, you can't get away with this."

Eddie waggled the little pistol admonishingly: "Don't be so self-righteous, Kennington. If *you* can get away with it, so can I! I know a respectable prostitute who will identify you as the man who threatened her with a gun last night. Oh yes, I know all about your movements—they've been so elephantine that all I've had to do since you've been in Paris has been to sit at home and plot them on the map with the aid of my pocket seismograph! Now sit down, be a good chap. If you make me nervous this thing might go off!"

"Raymond, will you sit down and stop this dangerous talk. Let's find out what Mr. Browne has on his mind."

"Thank you, Miss Canning." He leant forward and with his free hand slapped the pockets of my coat.

As I sat down I said to Josephine: "There's no reason to suppose this is anything but bluff. If anything happened to us, the dossier I've been working on would automatically reach the police. Mr. Browne is probably on their books already."

Eddie looked martyred: "The whole point of my bringing you both here is to prevent anything happening to you. But first things first—a drink, Miss Canning? . . . What about you, Kennington? . . . Oh all right, I'll have to drink alone."

When he had poured himself a stiff whiskey, he settled down in a chair, stretching out his long legs. The only indication that he wasn't quite so relaxed as he looked was the rubbing of one suede shoe against the other. But that, I decided, might have been due to chilblains.

"Now about this dossier of yours. I gather that you're working up a sensational crime-story that might prove damaging for trade with the Old Country: and the firm I represent have appointed me, as their English agent, to make a little *démarche* on their behalf. The fact is, your passion for playing the detective is stirring up a lot of mud: and frankly, if you don't stop, I wouldn't give two peas for your chances of survival. Now don't get me wrong. I personally detest all forms of violence, and it was entirely my idea to try and persuade you to see reason before it's too late. But I may say that my views prevailed by a very narrow margin. The Latins, you know, are very quick on the trigger. To put the matter in a nutshell, you know too much. What's more, you make a living out of selling your special knowledge to a wide public. You see what I mean?"

"Yes, I see. But how does Miss Canning come into it?"

"Ah, that's the whole essence of my plan. Though Miss Canning pretends to know nothing of all this, I'm afraid we must assume she does. So she comes into it on exactly the same footing as you do. If she talks, she signs your death-warrant as well as her own: and vice versa. And that's what really makes the scheme practicable—you'll keep each other out of mischief—each will feel responsible for the other. . . . You see, Miss Canning wasn't exaggerating when she called me a romantic! On my estimate, you're bound to listen to the voice of reason."

"And what does the voice of reason say?"

"You must drop the Millington-Forsett enquiry completely, and you mustn't attempt to work up your dossier for publication in any form whatsoever—let alone communicate any part of it to the police. . . . After all, that isn't much of a sacrifice, in return for a long and happy life. What do you think, Miss Canning?"

Josephine was apparently absorbed in lighting a cigarette. When she looked up she was smiling broadly. She got to her feet and stubbed out the cigarette.

"Women have no opinions," she said. "I think you two men would feel freer to bargain if you weren't constrained by the presence of a woman."

Eddie, no less surprised than I was, rose and followed her over to the door. Then, realizing that he still had his gun in his hand, slipped it into his pocket, murmuring politely: "No ill-feelings, I hope? May I wish you the best of luck?"

"That's very *sporting* of you, Mr. Browne!" Josephine turned and winked at me. "Raymond, I'll be waiting for you at the Rue d'Alger, and please don't be later than nine o'clock. We would *all* feel such fools if I had to come and rescue you with a Black Maria and a posse of policemen!"

CHAPTER TWELVE

The Workings of 'Destiny'

(1)

As the door closed, Eddie sighed. "Now, Kennington, what about a little snifter?"

"I'd love one, when you've put that gun away."

"As you wish"—he put it on the polished table, exactly between us, then pushed over the bottle and siphon. "Thirsty work!" he said. "This is on the *Maison*, so make it a good one!"

I took my time, while he watched me intently: with a trace of strain, I thought. Eventually I said: "Do you expect me to take all this seriously?"

"I don't see how you can do anything else. From Miss Canning's reactions to my little subterfuge, I gather the girl's in love with you, and though you don't look like a great lover, it wouldn't surprise me if the passion were mutual. You'll keep remembering you're up against a big international organization, and if you miscue, you'll feel hot breath down your neck, like a hunted character in one of your crime-books. . . ."

He went on building up the psychological situation. But I hardly listened. For the billiards metaphor he had just used had set up a very suggestive train of association—from Le Jockey, the billiards-playing waiter, to Charley's innocent reply to my advertisement: from my advertisement to the fact that Eddie read *The Times* in France. . . .

"Besides," Eddie concluded, "why risk your neck and Miss Canning's for Twight?"

"Why indeed?" I said. "But supposing we thought your

150

scheme was just bluff. Supposing we decided to call it? Wouldn't you be risking your neck too? I mean, wouldn't you be wise to reinsure yourself privately with me, so that if the police did somehow get hold of my dossier, they would at least have the facts, so far as you personally are concerned?"

Eddie looked at me strangely, tilting his long head backwards as though sniffing at the atmosphere. Then, without any warning from his facial muscles, he uttered the short contemptuous laugh of the man who isn't quite sure of himself.

"That's big of you, Kennington. But I don't think you need worry about me!"

"But I do! Perhaps you don't realize *how much* I know. I know, for instance, that the libel-case was cooked up between Millington-Forsett and Twight, and that subsequently Twight never got his cut. Either he was never intended to get it, or something happened afterwards that gave Milly the idea of murder—I'm referring of course to the LETTER . . . *You see, I know how that letter came to be written . . .*"

I paused for a drink and studied Eddie. He had started rubbing his feet together again, but his face was expressionless except for his habitual look of superiority. I could imagine him getting up from the mortuary table looking just like that —like a Zombie with an Old Etonian tie.

"Well?" Even now he couldn't resist baiting me. "I know you think you're a wizard detective. But if you really knew how that letter was written you'd be God Almighty!—even *you* couldn't know that. . . ."

He didn't realize the slip until I had jumped on him. "*Why do you think I couldn't know that?* I'll tell you why. Because you're the only living person who was present when Twight played the Suicide Game. You were in on the conspiracy from the beginning, and as far as I can gather you were in at the end, as Millington-Forsett's faithful lieutenant—yes, even on *La Futée*, where you only carried out the instructions of the Master. . . ."

As his hand moved towards the table, my foot came up under his side of it. I had been half expecting this eventuality, but my reaction was so nervously violent that siphon and bottle crashed to the floor, my glass upset in my lap, and the revolver skidded across the table to end up on the floor by my chair. I pounced on it, then stood up with whiskey pouring down my trouser-leg.

Eddie emerged from under the table with the siphon in one hand and the whiskey-bottle in the other. His forelock had detached itself and hung limply over his forehead. "I say, Kennington, that really was a bit thick. Can't a chap even make a pass at the bottle without being suspected of murderous intentions! Anyway, thank God there was a top on it! Now, what about filling up again?"

"Thanks, but you're the one who seems to need fortifying."

Eddie made no comment. He was engaged in refilling his own glass, which—I now noticed—had in fact been standing empty on the arm of his chair, half hidden by his hand. He sat back and took a long swig, reappraising me with a steady astonishment that reminded me of a child's, after some painful exhibition of parental caprice.

"You're a queer chap," he said at last. "You don't look as though you could knock the skin off a rice-pudding, yet here you are, living high detective fiction, convinced that you're outwitting a murderer!" . . . He broke off abruptly, listening. Then he got up and, moving swiftly and noiselessly across the room, snatched at the handle of the door.

There was nobody there—only a kitten playing with a bit of waste-paper—and he sat down again with a wintry self-deprecating smile. "Kennington, let's face it—you're not a detective and I'm not a murderer, but somehow we make each other nervous. If you like, I will tell you how and why Twight died. On one condition: that you first tell me how you know about the Suicide Game . . ."

(2)

. . . It was in 1925 that Eddie, swimming in a fiery sea of Irish whiskey, with the horse-copers, playwrights and political thugs who frequented Grady's bar in Dublin, first ran into 'Captain Davenport', who was then at the height of his career and looking out for a likely young man to help him with his Girls' Career Bureau. The meeting was 'providential', since Eddie had just then emerged from prison, without money or prospects, and with expensive tastes.

It was an organization after Eddie's heart. A good proportion of its profits were earned quite legally, because it really did 'place' its clients abroad ('as lady-dog exercisers, flower-arrangers and companions') and the girls who didn't like their jobs were the ones who were apt to lose their passports or get married to French citizens who suddenly disappeared. But through a cunning system of selection, aided by Natural Selection, most of them ultimately found themselves high up in the ancient profession which their looks, their adventurousness and the Bureau had written in their destiny. "They preferred," as Eddie put it, "to live in luxury rather than be their own mistresses!"

"Were the *Entreprise* and the Girls' Career Bureau one and the same?" I asked.

"Originally they were separate. But when Mattei cut up rough about a foreign firm operating on his territory, Milly agreed to combine forces—for a consideration, of course. Finally Mattei got Milly out altogether. But he only went because things were getting difficult his end. When the police eventually swooped, Milly had retired and was sitting pretty. But for political protection in France, Mattei might have found himself out of business too."

"What was your job exactly?"

"I was liaison officer between Mattei and Twight, and I also had to keep an eye on the Press. That was how I got to know Twight. He had written a sensational article about the pitfalls awaiting girls that went to work in France, and Milly considered him a potential menace. I went to see him, and decided he was a type who would do anything for money. So I introduced him to Milly. There were no more articles about pitfalls for girls. Within a few weeks he had published his famous article on the Travers case. And shortly after that I spent an evening with Twight at Milly's flat in Half Moon Street."

"That was the evening that took a morbid turn?"

"Morbid? We were all in roaring form, drinking and telling stories, and Milly, who was a bit of a dab at writing Limericks, insisted on showing off his talent. I remember the one he wrote about Johnny—it went something like this:

> *There was an old writer called Twight*
> *Whose bark was worse than his bite.*
> *His newspaper articles*
> *Tore people to particles,*
> *But the* damages *soon put them right!*

Anyway, that started the idea of paper-games. Milly was good at them and he loved showing off—he was a bit childish in some ways. Finally he said: 'Here's one you don't know. We used to play as children.' You can guess the rest?"

"Roughly. But I want the genesis of Twight's letter, as nearly as you can remember."

"I remember very well, because *the* letter was the final product of the first round, and Milly said it was a flop. It should have been more realistic! . . . Let me see . . . Oh yes, it was Milly that wrote: 'Journalist. Broken Heart': I wrote 'Stabs himself with Stylo Pen': and you know what Twight wrote . . ."

"And you suspected nothing at the time?"

"Absolutely nothing. After Twight went to France, Milly and I had a slight disagreement over an Irish girl-friend of mine who thought Milly would make a good sugar-daddy. One day, when we were alone, he asked me if I had seen Twight's first articles for the *Sunday Globe*. One of our girls had got linked with a French politician, which was just what we wanted to protect our interests. But Milly said he didn't trust Twight not to smell out this fact and write about it in the English press. What had happened, as I realized at once, was that Twight had threatened to use his knowledge of the Bureau if he didn't get his cut of the damages pretty quick. *Like you, he was dangerous to the Organization: and to Milly he was doubly dangerous.*

"Suddenly Milly said: 'Eddie, do you believe in Predestination?' 'Of course not,' I said, 'I'm a good Catholic.' 'Well, I do,' he said, 'and I've a p-p-premonition that our friend Johnny is going to c-c-commit suicide!'—you had to look out for yourself when you heard that slight stutter.

" 'How's he going to commit suicide?' I asked. 'Surely not with a stylo pen!'

"To my amazement, Milly was delighted with this remark: 'You're a brilliant boy, Eddie,' he said: 'and if you had a bit of capital, nothing could stop you being a millionaire. Now, if I've got to part with some of my capital, I'd rather you got it than Twight. Do you see what I'm driving at?' 'I think I do,' I said, 'but if the price of my getting capital is helping Twight to "fulfil his destiny", I'm afraid I'm not interested.' . . ."

Eddie had started pacing the room, and when I asked: "And did you warn Twight?" He twisted round and snapped at me:

"How could I? I'm not a bloody Salvationist. I took the risk of refusing Milly, and I took it knowing full well that he never accepted No for an answer . . ."

"You mean he tried to involve you in the drowning of Twight?"

"He *did* involve me. He made sure that if anything went wrong with his scheme, my head would qualify for the basket. . . ."

When I had got the whole story out of him, he said:

"Well? Are you satisfied?"

I said: "Since you're being so communicative, there is one last question I would like to put to you. If you're the sort of chap you've made yourself out to be—a chap who stops short of violence and murder—why the impulse to shoot me just now?"

He said: "My impulse was to fill up my glass. But you'll feel better about it if you go on thinking I wanted to shoot you!"

"That's all very fine, but people don't go about with loaded pistols unless they're prepared to shoot."

Eddie did not answer. But something about his expression caused me to pick up the gun and examine it. I fiddled with everything except the trigger till eventually I got it open. The chamber was completely empty!

I felt empty myself, shot off. And Eddie, observing this, immediately recovered his long-lost sneer:

"You've been hoist, so to speak, with your own petard!

But if I were you I wouldn't tell Miss Canning. She thinks you're a hero!"

(3)

When Josephine opened the door of Wildbore's flat, I realized at once that the stage was set. She was wearing a black full-skirted dress with a low neck, and she had combed out her hair, undoing the hairdresser's expensive work. Instead of asking me what had happened at Eddie's, she put out her hand and towed me without a word into the sitting-room, where there was a table laid for two with lobster-salad, fresh rolls and a bottle of champagne. A tray of drinks stood ready on the Louis Quinze *commode*.

"Stephen won't be back for four hours. Now go and get yourself a drink while I'm coping in the kitchen."

When she returned she was wearing Wildbore's maid's apron. She was singing softly to herself.

"So we've got four hours to ourselves!" I said nervously.

"Yes, we've got four hours to ourselves!"

"And tomorrow it'll all be over."

"What will be over?"

"Us, the Millington-Forsett enquiry—everything except Ricketts's cocktail party for the launching of that ill-starred book."

"Must it all be over? Have you decided that already?"

"You've decided, not me. I'm dull, smug and inhuman— you enjoy yourself better with people like Hugh, who know their onions about women."

"Raymond, you really are an ass!" Suddenly she was laughing. "But you are human after all! Were you really so angry about Hugh?"

"I had a right to be, didn't I? After all, you did come to Paris with me, knowing more or less how I feel about you."

"I did. And now I'll confess . . . I invented my little outing with Hugh, just to torment you. I simply have to do that sort of thing when I feel desperate. Have you ever heard of a female complaint called The Curse?"

I think it was the mention of the (for me) unmentionably intimate that made me realize how much I needed Josephine. I drew her on to the sofa beside me, and having posed her to my satisfaction, like a cut flower, I proceeded to make an owlish declaration.

She listened with compassion mixed with anguish. Then she said:

"Oh, Raymond, I never thought you'd be able to say it!"

"Then you *will*?"

"Perhaps . . . Can't we be just lovers until we know where we are?—till there's none of the old Canning and Kennington left, but just Josephine and Raymond?"

"You mean you don't love me . . . enough?"

She shook her head violently, so that her hair fanned out, to settle dishevelled round the nape of her small white neck: "The trouble is, you don't say anything about your own feelings. All this began so improbably: it was worked up by a designing female: and now we're involved in obscure, threatening circumstances that won't let us be ourselves. . . ."

I said: "Obscure, yes. But threatening, I wonder. Eddie started by menacing us *on behalf of his gang*, but later, when he discovered what I had on him personally, he wasn't so gang-minded any more. He told me practically everything he had apparently been trying to prevent me finding out, just to insure his own neck. You know, it wouldn't surprise me if this whole gang build-up turned out to be Eddie's private invention for coping with a simple, impressionable crime-writer. . . ."

Josephine said quietly: "I wish you really believed that: I

can't. When Eddie went out to get you, and left me in that room with a huge thug standing guard in the doorway, I had plenty of time to think things over. It was bad enough to be suddenly rung up and told you had had a street accident. But when I got to the hospital and found Eddie waiting for me, I had an even worse shock. 'As far as I know,' Eddie told me, 'Kennington hasn't had his "accident" yet. But he's been *sentenced to death*, and now your only chance of saving him is to co-operate with me.' What's more, I believe he really meant it. . . . No, darling, it may all be a clever bluff, but I don't want to go through that again—ever. . . . In fact"— she made a queer little gesture, and suddenly her whole self seemed concentrated in her eyes—"in fact, I *will* marry you. . . ."

It took a moment for this to sink in. Then I said suspiciously: "But you don't love me—except in this context?"

"Oh, Raymond, you're impossible! Didn't I say 'let's be lovers'? How can I say what you want me to say while you're still backing against the end of the sofa like a stone-wall batsman on a sticky wicket! Don't you see, that's why I wanted you as a lover . . . there was, there still is, no other way of penetrating your thick hide! . . ."

We were at the coffee stage, discussing marriage, when Josephine had a bright idea: "I say, why don't we turn Ricketts's ramp into a romance by announcing our engagement at the cocktail party? As we re-launch Millington-Forsett on the world, we'll wash our hands of him for ever. We might even have a ceremonial burning of the *dossier*, so that if there are any spies present, disguised as reviewers or crime-reporters, they'll see for themselves there's no deception!"

That facetious suggestion had the effect of a sermon after

the singing. Realizing this herself, Josephine said: "And *à propos*, now that we've got to share the risk of assassination, I want to know what you've added to that *dossier*." She got up, kicked off her shoes and settled down on the floor beside me with her legs tucked comfortably under the sweep of her skirt. "And I've a *right* to know what you were doing, threatening a respectable prostitute!"

I was near the end of the story when she said: "Wait a minute. Do you really believe yourself that Milly would have risked his whole plan just to involve Eddie in it?"

I said: "I was just coming to that. You see, at the time of the Suicide Game, the plan was already roughed out and Eddie was the corner-stone of it, because of his passion for motor-boats. But Milly didn't try to sell his plan to Eddie until it was practically ripe for execution. By which time Mattei had been tipped off that Twight was a menace to the racket, and that in view of the existence of a suicide-for-love letter, and of the Bureau's facilities for providing the lady, his death could be arranged without risk."

"But why the motor-boat idea in the first place? It seems a cumbrous way of faking a suicide by drowning."

"That's what I thought too when I stumbled on *La Futée*. Then I realized the significance of the mark on Twight's ankle. I remembered an accident on the Thames in 1928, which caused a stir because the victim was about to have a very inconvenient child. She was coiling up a warp in the stern of a motor-boat when her 'lover' unexpectedly trod on the accelerator and she went over with the rope caught round her ankle. His story was that the engine and the wash were making such a din, that he didn't realize what had happened till he had dragged her for some minutes, feet up, head down, against the current. What must have struck Milly about the case—criminals notoriously get inspiration from the news-papers—was the pathologist's evidence at the inquest, which saved him from a murder charge: it was that *water, suddenly forced into the lungs under pressure, produces shock and speeds up the process of drowning. . . ."*

I had my arm round Josephine's shoulders and I suddenly realized she was shivering. She took the glass of brandy I gave her and swallowed all of it at a gulp. She choked and put her hand to her breast; but she wasn't shivering any more when she said: "I don't really want to hear the details. But there's one thing I must know—how did they manage to involve Eddie against his will?"

"That was the diabolical part of it, the fruit of Milly's last visit to Paris, when he saw Mattei behind Eddie's back. It was Eddie, in full agreement with Mattei's instructions, who organized the Twight-Marcelline *liaison*. It was Eddie who then got the job of sacking Marcelline, ostensibly for failing to worm herself into Twight's affairs. And when Mattei suddenly and mysteriously announced that he was going to 'do a deal' with Twight, it was again Eddie, the diplomat, who was given the delicate task of bringing Twight to a night rendezvous at Mattei's house on the river."

"And Twight never got there?"

"It happened when they were crossing on their way back to Paris."

"Crossing?"

"They had left the car on the other side of the river. Mattei's chauffeur said the road was being repaired on the land side. Twight was full of brandy and satisfaction: his interview with Mattei had been highly successful, both from a crook's and a journalist's point-of-view. There was no moon and that part of the river was completely deserted. Mattei's boatman, who was to bring the *Futée* home, insisted on Eddie taking the wheel, so that he could appreciate a new type of propeller Mattei had installed. They were in midstream when Twight's hat was knocked off. As he leant over to grab it, the boatman pushed his head down, while the chauffeur lifted up his legs. Eddie felt the violent rocking of the boat, but he didn't realize Twight had gone overboard till a voice told him to switch on the searchlight and put the wheel hard over. Eddie wanted to stop dead and swivel the searchlight round. But the searchlight wouldn't swivel: with the result, no doubt carefully calculated, that he had to keep going ahead, searching for Twight in widening circles. Twight, meanwhile, was being dragged astern by a short rope—the chauffeur had tried to slip a canvas noose over both his legs, but had only succeeded in getting it over one. By the time Eddie realized what had happened, Twight had 'fulfilled his destiny', and Eddie had fulfilled his. There was nothing between him and the scaffold but to help Mattei's minions erase the two possible blots on the immaculate 'suicide':—to haul Twight up and go through his pockets: and to recuperate his cocky little Tyrolese hat. By that time Eddie didn't need to be told that Twight's letter had been sent off to Marcelline. . . ."

"Yet he went on working for this gang?"

"I don't think he's a very courageous man, and he had been superbly framed. Mattei, you see, pretended not to believe that Eddie didn't know the nature of the 'deal' Twight was going to get. Milly had given Mattei to understand that Eddie was completely *au courant*. He had also said: 'But you'd better not give him any chance to back out of it—the poor boy has such a tender conscience!' . . ."

During the silence that followed, my heart started a violent commentary. Or was it Josephine's? It no longer seemed possible to distinguish.

Presently she whispered: "Whatever happens now, at least there are two of us."

It was my duty not to let that pass unchallenged. But my answer was in two distinct parts.

I pointed out that Millington-Forsett was dead, and that the metal of his successors apparently had a lower melting point.

Then I took her back to my hotel. The night-porter winked at me. But I no longer felt like kicking him in the teeth.

CHAPTER THIRTEEN

The Cocktail Party

"WELL, WELL!" exclaimed Mrs. Roddie, at seven o'clock the following evening, "I hardly recognized you, Mr. Kennington!" And when she had looked from my trousers to my face, and then back again to the whiskey stains: "I see you've had a nice time in Paris. They tell me it's a very gay city! I suppose you'll be wanting your dinner just as usual. I had rabbit pie waiting for you last night, and now you'll just have to eat it warmed up!"

I said: "Rabbit pie improves with warming up. Goodness, I'm glad to be home again. Now if you'll come up to my room for a quick one, I'll let you into a little secret."

"I should have thought *you'd* had enough alcohol. But I don't mind coming up for a nip, when I've put the pie back into the oven."

I gave her a glass of the port I kept specially for her, and as soon as she showed signs of weakening, I weighed in with the bottle of powerful scent which Josephine, maliciously and with aforethought, had bought for her at the Gare du Nord.

She took the stopper off, retracting a corner of her upper lip as though inhaling garlic for the first time. Then she coughed and said: "You must have taken leave of your senses, Mr. Kennington, buying pairfume for an old crow like me. I doubt the French girruls have been giving you notions!"

She was obviously delighted, and I decided that this was my cue:

"What would you say if I told you I was engaged to be married?"

"It would confirrm my opinion that you'd taken leave of your senses!"

She looked at me warily, lighting another cigarette from the previous one.

"Well, I suppose it's better to marry than to burrn . . . but I can see you're only teasing me, Mr. Kennington."

"I promise I'm not teasing you. This time I've gone and got myself properly engaged."

"To one of them French feemuls?"

"*NO*, to an English girl. She came here one night recently, and she would have come again if she hadn't been so scared of you."

"Oh, that one. Well, at least she's not a foreigner, and she *talks* like a lady. . . ." She took out her handkerchief and blew her nose loudly. "Well, dear, I won't say but it won't be a great pairshonal loss to me, but I wish you both luck with all my heart . . . now what about a wee drop more port? . . ."

Next morning Ricketts telephoned that he wanted to see me urgently. Could I come round to the office about three?

Fearing some sinister development I got hold of Josephine during the lunch-hour and was soothed to hear that it was only the cocktail party Ricketts was worried about.

It seemed that the House of Hodge and Ricketts was divided against itself. Though Hodge had been persuaded that such low publicity stunts were henceforth inevitable if the firm was to be saved from the greedy maw of Heintz and Mitchens, he didn't disguise his opinion that Ricketts's plans for the launching of *A Twist Somewhere* were another step on the downward progress that had begun when they accepted my first book. Ricketts badly needed my support.

He had not told Hodge that I was coming. But Josephine gave the show away, and I had hardly shaken hands with Ricketts before Hodge came marching into his room, followed by Josephine wearing dark glasses and looking just as

I had imagined *La Futée* would look before I discovered that she was a motor-boat.

Hodge tried delaying tactics, pretending to be impatient to hear all about the discoveries I had made in Paris. Josephine, as agreed, had kept silent on that subject, and I endorsed her silence by saying that I couldn't give a proper account until I had put all my notes in order. That gave Ricketts his chance.

"Well now, Ray, Miss Canning probably told you about the circus we're putting on for your book. John here doesn't much like the idea—and of course I respect his scruples—but he does see the sales angle and we've agreed on a date ten days hence, which will be just in time to get the Christmas book-trade before it reaches saturation point. But that means we've got to hurry and decide exactly what sort of a party we're going to throw. Now I don't know what *you* think, but as I see it, there's no use my lining up reviewers, crime-reporters and gossip-writers unless we've got something more to offer them than gin—those fellows can get gin any night of the week at a dozen parties. . . ."

Hodge said: "There you go again. I still don't see what's the matter with sherry." Having already conceded the main position, he was still skirmishing over minor details. "We want to give them the 'dope" as you insist on calling it, but we don't want them to be *doped*—we want to sell them Raymond's book."

"All right then—sherry if you like. But you know that's not what I'm talking about. What I mean is: we've got to offer them a show—and that's where Ray comes in. To meet these press-boys we want people who've helped him over the Millington-Forsett case. We want Patterson and Pusey, and—what's the name of that fellow from Scotland Yard? And Moxon, the mystery-man from Brixton, who actually knew

Mr. Percy Shelley . . . even at a pinch the Irish landlady. Do you think you could get hold of those people, Ray?"

Hodge said cynically: "Why not ask Mrs. Danby too?"

"Well, Ray?" Ricketts ignored Hodge completely.

I said: "All but Pusey would probably be glad to come."

"Good man! I thought you'd approve. Now what about the gamekeeper you interviewed? He's the only person remotely connected with the Travers case. Could you get him to come along too?"

Hodge said: "Raymond didn't say he approved. And even if he does I absolutely veto the gamekeeper."

I said: "I don't think he would come anyway."

"Well, then, who else is there? We can't risk the thing falling flat. . . ." Ricketts puffed at his pipe for a minute. Then his gaze wandered from me to Josephine.

"I've got it! Why don't we introduce a spot of romance? Miss Canning and Raymond get together on the Millington-Forsett case, and when it's over they find they can't live apart. Sorry that's not better expressed, but you get the general idea? If Miss Canning would . . . er, lend herself, we could announce an engagement at the party!"

He lobbed this grenade into our midst as innocently as a child with a stinkbomb.

Hodge said: "Oh, for God's sake, Arthur. You're utterly shameless! Miss Canning's my secretary and I'm certainly not prepared to let her 'lend herself' to any low-down publicity stunt. About that Raymond will agree with *me*."

"I certainly do." I spoke with feeling. And then I saw that Josephine was blushing, the sort of blush that reveals a young girl's guilty passion for a married man old enough to be her father. She tried to save her face with a smile, but realizing that it wasn't convincing, she went an even deeper shade of crimson. There was nothing for it but to step in and make an honest woman of her.

"I'm sorry, but it so happens that Josephine and I really are engaged, and we don't want any publicity—of *that* sort."

Ricketts upset his chair as he started up from behind his desk. "My God!" he roared, "you're not really? Miss Canning, take off those hideous glasses—I've always wanted an excuse to kiss you."

His hide was so thick, his enthusiasm so genuine, that Hodge had to stop looking as though he wanted to jump out of the window. He shook us both by the hand. "You're a sly dog, Raymond!" he said, and Josephine squeezed my arm: "Yes, he's more *futé* than one would think."

"So that's settled." Ricketts triumphantly forgot what I had said. "With a real romance we can't go wrong. Sherry won't do now. We'll have to have champagne cocktails."

"It's *not* settled. We're keeping it secret until the wedding anniversary of Josephine's parents. . . ."

We all turned and looked at Josephine, who was now perched on the edge of the desk, describing circles in the air with an elegant toe.

"Well!" she said—and I knew before she spoke that Ricketts's kiss had changed her mind. "Well, I *did* think of it myself *actually* . . . after all, if it hadn't been for Millington-Forsett . . ."

"Josephine," said Ricketts, "you were born to make good men happy."

Pusey, as I had predicted, found himself too out of touch with the literary world to venture back into it. But Bairstow said patronizingly: "If the exigencies of the service permit, I would be delighted to look in and wish your book *bon voyage*." And Patterson: "So it's safe to take the lid off the hot-pot at last? I wouldn't miss the feast for worlds!" Moxon's letter was as follows: "You can't imagine, my dear Mr. Kennington, how flattered I am that you have followed up the clues I gave you and laid the ghost of Mr. Percy Shelley. It will be an honour to join with you in drinking another toast to our friend in the shades, coupled with one to *A Twist Somewhere*, for which I have already placed my order."

I had never been the hero of any hour. I had never had a book 'launched', nor had an engagement announced publicly. So when the night came I primed myself with whiskey at the Temple Bar restaurant before mounting to the first floor landing of Hodge and Ricketts, where a table of drinks had been installed with the Production Manager as barman. The partners were already receiving guests and Josephine was deep in conversation with a well-known crime-reporter. "You're late!" Ricketts whispered to me. "There's an old boy coming up the stairs behind you who looks as though he might be on the bridegroom's side."

It was Moxon, wearing a black suit with four buttons on the coat, craning his head over a butterfly collar that looked as though it were made of celluloid. "Mr. Kennington," he panted, "I saw you *emerge* ahead of me and did my best to catch you up. I hope I am not unpunctual, for this is a treat far beyond the wildest dreams of a poor old crock like me."

"Mr. Moxon, these are my publishers—Mr. Hodge . . . and Mr. Ricketts . . ."

As I went to get Moxon a brandy and soda, I heard Ricketts say, "Very kind of you, Sir. I understand we're already specially indebted to you for making this little party possible." When I came back Moxon was being introduced to a new arrival, a dapper little man with rimless glasses. "Mr. Moxon, this is Mr. Geoffrey Kirkwood. You may perhaps know him as Juryman of the *Daily Post?*"

"Moxon?"—Kirkwood searched his memory of crime and criminals and was quickly put right by Ricketts—"Mr. Moxon got us out of a nasty threat of libel by enabling us to trace Millington-Forsett . . . he had the pleasure of knowing him personally . . ."

Ricketts was doing the work of two men. Hodge lurked on the fringes of small groups, trying to look detached from the ignoble proceedings. I took a fiendish pleasure in introducing him to Bairstow: "This is Detective Inspector Bairstow of Scotland Yard. He specializes in dragging muddy rivers for corpses."

"Oh, really?" Hodge shifted his ivory cigarette-holder to the other side of his mouth and gazed into Bairstow's well-scrubbed face with a look of keen bewilderment.

"Friend Kennington will have his little joke. But we policemen rather enjoy a bit of ragging from the detective-story merchants!"

The party was beginning to go. The skilful introductions of Ricketts had started conversations here and there between members of the Press and the 'bridegroom's guests'. Having nothing in common but Millington-Forsett, the two groups had nothing else to discuss. Some of them drifted into Ricketts's room, where copies of *A Twist Somewhere* were laid out like Bibles for public edification. I went in there to look for Josephine, whom I wanted to introduce to Patterson. I found her listening, entranced, to a noble gossip-writer explaining why my books fell between two stools. "Here *is* Raymond Kennington!" she said blandly, and the peer, quickly consulting his watch, said: "Well, I'm afraid I must be getting on—I've two other parties tonight. Goodbye!"

Josephine said: "He's brilliant at slinking out of tight corners. Look at him edging for the stairs behind Ricketts's back."

But he didn't get further than the landing, for Ricketts chose that moment to shout: "Attention please! Will you all fill up your glasses—I've got an important announcement to make."

There was a general scramble towards the bar and we watched the peer hesitate on the stairhead, torn between the desire to escape and the fear of missing an item for his column. His hesitation was fatal, for at that moment Moxon clutched him by the arm, and shortly afterwards, when silence fell upon the gathering, was heard saying loudly: "Delightful man. The Ballarneys were all judges of horseflesh . . ."

"Gentlemen . . . and Miss Canning," Ricketts began, "for a little publisher's this is a big evening, and since I'm the junior partner with the big voice, I've been asked to say a few words in connection with the book we're publishing to-morrow . . . Now don't think I'm trying to sell you anything! [laughter]—there isn't a Twist anywhere as far as the author or his publishers are concerned! [renewed laughter]. . . . But thereby hangs a tale! [Cries of 'Cut it short'.] We wouldn't be publishing this book at all, if the author, assisted by some of you here tonight, hadn't done a brilliant bit of detective work and traced Claude Nevil Millington-Forsett to his final resting-place in Marylebone. I might add that in the course of his investigations in Paris he's made a discovery that's going to cause . . ."

Josephine and I had been exchanging hooded looks like two cobras swaying helplessly to the strains of some monotonous wind-instrument. This was too much. I interrupted Ricketts in mid-sentence: "As this is rather personal, do you mind if I say a word?"

"Go ahead, Raymond. You're the man they want to hear."

I said: "What Arthur Ricketts was going to say, when I

rudely interrupted him, was that during the course of the investigation I made a discovery that's going to revolutionize my life. If it hadn't been for Josephine Canning—she's the only woman here tonight, so you know who I mean—I shouldn't have got anywhere as an amateur detective. And if it hadn't been for her it would never have occurred to me that I was heartily sick of being a bachelor. I only want to say . . . well, what about another drink?"

They crowded round, drinking our health and congratulating us.

It was only when I broke out of the circle to refill my own glass that I noticed a new arrival standing at the stairhead talking to Ricketts.

He was a small man wearing a black frock-coat, green with age and far too big for him. He had a red carnation in his buttonhole. In his hand was a copy of *A Twist Somewhere*. Ricketts came dashing up. "Champagne for one of your guests. He says his name is Gordon Byron."

I took one look, then I seized Josephine and whispered fiercely in her ear. "For Christ's sake get hold of Moxon quickly and ask him if he knows that old man."

"Mr. Gordon Byron?"—I interrupted his reading of *A Twist Somewhere*.

"Why yes, Mr. Kennington. I gather I'm just in time to congratulate you on your engagement. I wish I could also congratulate you on your latest publication . . . *but I fear that might be p-p-premature!*"

My glass fell out of my hand, and almost simultaneously I heard Moxon's voice. "Shelley, by God, I want fifty pounds or I'll have the law on you."

"Surely there must be some mistake?" said the newcomer, looking Moxon up and down with distaste. "I don't think I've had the pleasure of meetin' you."

CHAPTER FOURTEEN

Millington-Forsett?

"I'M BEWILDERED by all this revelry!" said Mr. Gordon Byron, *alias* Percy Shelley. "I . . . I just dropped in for a little talk with your publishers."

"Were they expecting you?" I asked.

Mr. Byron heaved, twisting his shoulders. From his eyes, which were prominent and bluish-green, I concluded that he had laughed.

"I understood from *advance publicity* that they were bringin' out a book of special interest to me. Mr. Ricketts put the book in my hand, and now I've had time to glance at it, I'm quite sure that they will be interested in the little proposal I have to make. But there's no hurry, no hurry at all. My dear boy, run away and amuse yourself."

"Could you possibly wait half an hour or so? Perhaps"—somehow I had to get him out of the way. "Perhaps you would wait in the Production Manager's office. What would you like to drink?"

"That's decent, very decent of you. For some years I've been on the wagon, but in view of *this* occasion . . ."

I led him into Cutts's office and installed him in a leather armchair. Then I shut the door and went back to the party.

Hodge went a shade greyer when I told him of our visitor and warned me to say nothing to anybody, above all to keep the Press away from Cutts's room. I said: "Moxon has identified him as Shelley, but he seems not to know Moxon. Anyway, until we've had a talk with him, there's no reason to start panicking. I'm going to have a word with Patterson."

I found Patterson studying a portrait of Hodge's father.

"You saw that old man with the buttonhole and the frock coat?"

Patterson dug me slyly in the third waistcoat button. "I've seen some publicity stunts in my time, but this beats them all hollow. Why, he's the living image of Millington-Forsett. Was it your publishers' idea?"

"Mr. Patterson, this isn't a publicity stunt. None of us know anything about him. I don't see how he *can* be Millington-Forsett. But if he *is*, then we're in a god-awful mess. Until we've made sure, you can help us by keeping it under your hat."

Patterson whistled, more with his bronchi than with his lips. "Of course I could easily be mistaken. Isn't there any relative who could identify him for certain?"

I snapped my fingers and went to find Josephine. "Listen, darling, at least two people here are prepared to swear that the old man with the buttonhole is Millington-Forsett. As soon as we've got rid of this party, Hodge, Ricketts and I are going to find out what he's come for. It may be just a practical joke somebody's trying to pull on us. But if it isn't, the first thing is to check his identity, and the only way of doing that is to get hold of Mrs. Danby, quickly. Will you wait in Hodge's room while we're talking to him, and if I ring through and say: 'Josephine, I'm sorry I can't dine tonight', get into a taxi and go and get her. . . . I think she'll come all right if you handle her tactfully and switch on the charm. . . ."

It was like the Red Death from the plague-stricken city turning up at the Prince's frivolous masked ball. From the anxious demeanour of the hosts, the guests seemed to gather that something had gone wrong and hung about expecting sensational developments. I laughed myself hoarse trying to appear in high spirits, and when somebody asked me about 'the old man in fancy dress', I said: "Oh, it's the phantom at the feast! As a matter of fact he's an old actor who's trying to get Hodge to publish his memoirs."

Moxon, himself a spectral figure, came up behind me when I was getting a drink, and clutched my arm with bony fingers. He seemed ghoulishly excited by the situation, muttering, winking, and shaking his head: "Did you see Shelley's face when I spoke to him! Gordon Byron indeed! . . . rich, isn't it?"

I said: "Last time I met you, you were perfectly confident that he was dead. How do you account for his remarkable recovery?"

"Didn't you say yourself that old soldiers never die? To me the whole thing is unnatural, bordering on the supernatural. Deuced awkward for me as well as you."

"Why awkward for you, Mr. Moxon?"

"Because I feel, if I may say so, profoundly associated with you and the fortunes of your book. I am responsible for encouraging you in the first place. I imagine Shelley hasn't come here for nothing."

When the guests were all gone, Hodge said grimly: "Now for it, Raymond. If this individual is the man he seems to be —well, I hope you've got your answers ready, that's all." Even Ricketts was hostile behind his jocularity. "You're a bloody fine detective, you are!"

As we entered Cutts's room, the Millington-Forsett figure rose to his feet ceremoniously. "How good of you to find time to see me at this festive hour!"

Hodge said with terrible courtesy: "I'm sorry we've kept you waiting so long. If you had only thought of making an appointment . . ."

The little man shrugged his shoulders, so that his coat hung on him like a scarecrow's. "Appointments? I'm too old for that sort of thing. With one foot in the grave and lackin' the necessary, I have plenty of patience to wait for the busy young people who run the world nowadays."

Hodge ignored this bit of philosophy: "Now, Mr. Byron, I understand you have a business proposition to make?"

"Er, yes, I have. I have indeed. But before I make it, I would like to sort out you three gentlemen. You, young man"—he fixed Hodge with a terrible stare—"are the senior partner in this publishin' house? And you, with the pipe, are the junior partner? Mr. Kennin'ton I have already identified from the photograph on the back of his book. Well, then, now we know each other. . . ."

I interrupted: "I'm sorry, but we still don't know *you*."

"All right, all right. But first let me wet my whistle."

When he had wetted his whistle—the phrase struck me as ominously authentic—he took one of Cutts's cigars off the desk and, sniffing it quickly with raised eyebrows, replaced it in the box: "H'm, good cigars, eh? Signs of prosperity?"

He opened his copy of *A Twist Somewhere* and tapped a marked page with the monocle suspended by a black thread from his buttonhole: "I suppose you expect to make a lot out of this book. Five thousand pounds? . . . perhaps ten thousand wouldn't be an over-estimate? . . . Come now, Mr. Hodge, don't shake your head so modestly. All this noise and publicity tells me you have high hopes."

Hodge made a strangled noise and Ricketts had to speak up for him. "It certainly would be an over-estimate. Publishing involves *risk*, great risk. Some books sell, others don't. It's no trade secret that on a book of essays like this a publisher will be extremely lucky if he grosses five hundred pounds to share with the author. What you describe as 'all this noise and publicity' is in fact a cheap substitute for expensive advertisements in newspapers."

"I agree," said Hodge. "However, all this is academic. You forget you are still a complete stranger to us."

Mr. Byron said: "Oh, come! A complete stranger? I should have thought that Mr. Kennin'ton at any rate would have pierced my poetic disguise by now."

I said: "The poetic disguise seems to have two layers. Mr. Moxon, whom you apparently don't know, identifies you as 'Mr. Percy Shelley'. But you want us to think that you are Mr. Claude Nevil Millington-Forsett."

"I don't want you to *think* anything, my boy. If you had done your work conscientiously, you would *know* that I am *Millington-Forsett.** And since you propose to make money by accusin' me of committin' a murder, I propose to cash in on your profits in advance . . . and I want them at once without any shillyshallyin' . . . No, NO!"—he silenced us with a five-pronged stab of his hand and the flash of a gold signet-ring—"this is a disgraceful attack on an innocent man, and if you refuse my terms of peace, I shall have no mercy on you . . . I shall bring you down, as I brought Twight down . . . I shall bring you down into the gutter. . . ."

His voice had risen almost to a scream, and the effect on Hodge was so demoralizing that when I said quickly: "But you won't get us in the *river*!" Hodge murmured miserably: "Really, Raymond, is that sort of remark worth while?"

In the pause that followed Hodge and Ricketts both looked at me for inspiration. I looked at my watch. "Excuse me," I said, with what must have seemed like remarkable coolness under fire, " I must just telephone Josephine—she's waiting to be taken out to dinner and it looks as if I'd better put her off."

But when I replaced the receiver, the tinkling and crackling of the instrument betrayed the shakiness of my hand. I looked

* He pronounced it Millinton-Fosset.

177

at the old man and said: "If you really are Millington-Forsett, why this generous proposal? Wouldn't you do better to wait and sue us? In the Twight case the jury awarded enormous damages."

There were sounds of Josephine leaving rapidly, and Mr. Byron cocked his head, listening. Then he sighed, apparently exhausted by his histrionics.

"How old are you, Mr. Kennin'ton? . . . Fortyish, eh? Well, suppose you live to be eightyish, do you suppose you would feel like suin' anybody? . . . So many days sittin' on hard benches, tryin' to keep awake in case some idiot asks you a question: such a fuss and bother and expense! Of course I would get my expenses paid, and after months of arguin' I would be awarded an enormous capital sum. But would I live to spend it, and—what's more important—would you be able to pay up? You are doin' well, I fancy, but you're not as prosperous as all that. No, gentlemen, I'd rather have a bit of pocket-money . . . have a heart now, please. Don't force me to sue you."

I said: "Believe me, that's the last thing we want. But don't you see, any charlatan might come along here pretending to be Millington-Forsett, trying to frighten us into paying up quickly? Mr. Byron, I think I'm speaking for my publishers as well as myself when I say that until you've proved your identity beyond a shadow of doubt, there can be no question of paying you a penny."

Mr. Byron rose with some difficulty, pulling himself up with his hands crossed over the silver knob of his walking-stick. He stood beside the desk flicking over the pages of *A Twist Somewhere*. Then he picked up the book and tossed it into the waste-paper basket.

"Well," he said, moving towards the door, "well, Messrs. Hodge, Ricketts and Kennin'ton—I've given you a sportin' chance. But you seem determined to bring down this House . . . an old family business, I should imagine . . ."

"Sit down, please sit down." Hodge passed his hand over his forehead. "Mr. Kennington does *not* speak for his publishers. What sum of money did you have in mind?"

"A thousand pounds, and I want it in cash, together with a written statement that in view of the gross attack you have made on my honour, you, the author and publishers of this book, freely acknowledge your liability to that extent. If you do this at once, without fuss, I am prepared to sign a paper promising not to take any legal action. I'd even be prepared to let the book come out!"

He chuckled hideously at that idea, and I said: "Just one more question, Mr. Byron. If I have, as you allege, made a disgraceful attack on an innocent man, how do you explain away what the gamekeeper at Pulbury told his son about the pheasant getting up *behind* you? . . . I presume you've read the end of the essay?"

I thought for a second that he didn't know what I was talking about. Then he began to shake with laughter that was more like a dry spasm of coughing: "I marked that bit, because I could see you had enjoyed writin' it! And now I'll tell you something that will really amuse you. . . . A pheasant *did* get up behind me, and it would have been devilish awkward for me if Thompson had refused the money I offered him not to blow the gaff!" He leant over the desk, still shaking with laughter over the memory, while the three of us stared at him in horrified amazement. . . .

"So you *did* murder Travers?" I managed to say, when I had sufficiently recovered to be able to speak.

He started, as though suddenly aware of where he was and whom he was talking to. "Of course I didn't. . . . What do you take me for! The pheasant got up after I had fired the shot. It was a hen, and the one I fired at was a cock. A gorgeous bird, too. Pity it got up in line with Travers!"

Since the first shock of Byron's appearance, I had gradually convinced myself that he wasn't really Millington-Forsett. Something theatrical about the man, a feeling that he wasn't sinister enough, had given me assurance to challenge him and to keep on challenging. Now I had nothing more to say. The affair was in the hands of Hodge and Ricketts; and Hodge, I could see, was beginning to think a thousand pounds would be well spent in buying himself out of this nightmare. . . .

"Good, then," Mr. Byron was saying, "my representative, a tall man with a white buttonhole, will be waiting at eleven outside the Pall Mall entrance to Lloyds. He will take the money and hand you my letter agreeing to the settlement. I need hardly say that any attempt on your part . . ."

The telephone rang and I went to Ricketts's room, to which I had myself switched the line. It was Josephine, slightly husky with smoking and excitement: "Is he still there? Can you hang on to him half an hour longer? . . . she says she'll come, provided she doesn't have to meet 'that sinister young man'—you! But she's completely bats, and may change her mind any moment."

"Where are you ringing from?"

"A call-box near Stamford Bridge—I've slipped out to get some food for Mrs. Danby's cats . . . she says she can't leave them with empty stomachs, and anyway she has to change into her Sunday best."

I said: "Damn! I can hear the old man going, and if I don't follow we may lose him completely. You'd better bring her to the Temple Bar restaurant. Give her food and drink, and be passionately interested in cat-Caesarians . . . Yes, I'll ring as soon as I've run him to earth . . . what? . . . of course I do, darling, what a question! . . ."

The Partners were outside on the landing, whispering amid cigarette ends and broken glass. I tiptoed past them with my finger to my lips and looked over the banisters. As soon as I heard the front door swing, I made history in Hodge and Ricketts. I slid down the banisters.

Mr. Byron didn't look his age from behind. Despite his stoop he walked with surprising briskness, and once, on the stretch between the lawcourts and St. Clement Dane's, he stopped leaning on his stick and swung it gaily. There were a number of pedestrians, and in my anxiety not to lose sight of him I came quite close, to find him standing on the curb peering back in my direction. I had dodged into a doorway before I realized that he had no idea he was being followed. He was only looking to see whether his bus, which was coming up, would get to the bus-stop before him.

Reading detective novels I am always astonished by the ease with which 'shadows' do their work in cities. If there hadn't been a succession of buses together I should certainly have lost Mr. Byron within a few hundred yards of the starting point. The bus he boarded was a Ninety-Four, and the one behind it, which I boarded, was due to diverge at Charing Cross. It was by a sheer fluke that mine followed his closely to Charing Cross, and that I happened to see him get off at Lyons Corner House, pause to buy an evening paper, and then scurry off down a side-street. By the time I got off he had disappeared, but the alley he had entered was a blind one, with two public houses in it, and an establishment called the Trafalgar Sherry Dive.

I plumped for the Trafalgar Sherry Dive, for no sounder reason than that my puritan mind associated 'dives' with vice.

It was one of Ye Olde Tudor bars, with panelling and oaken doors. I was peering round one of the enormous pillars, when a door marked GENTS creaked just behind me and he came trotting out, buttoning his frock-coat, and passed within a foot of me.

The place was crowded. The drinkers stood three-deep at the bar and drinks were being passed over the heads of the front row. I watched Mr. Byron approach and stand for a minute on the fringe of the scrum, wondering how he was going to get a drink. Then, very deliberately, he raised his stick and poked a young man in the small of the back. In a moment he was cleaving his way through a breach in the astonished wall of beery humanity amid cries of 'Don't mind us!' and 'Go it, dad!'

Presently he emerged with a tankard of beer, and sitting down at a table set for dinner against one of the central pillars, began studying the Gothick menu. A waiter went past, run off his feet, and he too received a poke in the back. As he turned to protest, Byron fixed him with his monocle. There was a sharp argument, but eventually the waiter shrugged his shoulders and took the order with bad grace.

I caught the waiter going through a swing door. "Would you like to earn ten bob?" I asked. "Right then . . . that old man whose order you've just taken—do you think you could make his meal last three-quarters of an hour?"

"He'll be lucky if he gets his grub tonight, the old b——r. He seems to think this is the Ritz 'otel."

"Good. Now tell me where your telephone is."

I waited twenty minutes, then rang the Temple Bar restaurant. Josephine had just arrived.

When I came back to my observation-point I thought for a moment that my waiter had let me down. Byron was completely hidden by a broad back I didn't recognize. I made my way discreetly to a better station. Then I saw that there were two people sitting with him.

One was Moxon and the other was Mrs. Kernan.

I was still speculating about the meaning of this powerful combination when—a quarter of an hour later—Mrs. Danby and Josephine came down the stairs and stood irresolute at the foot of them. Josephine was grasping the old lady's arm like a woman policeman. Mrs. Danby looked wilder than ever and completely bewildered. She was wearing an extraordinary little fur hat which perched on her hair like a rat resting on a truss of hay.

Josephine saw me just in time. I pointed towards the Byron table and made signs that she wasn't to recognize me. She piloted Mrs. Danby to a table within full view of the trio. Then I saw her lean over and say something in a low voice.

Of what followed I expected to see no more than a silent version. But the sound-track came on with a crash. Mrs. Danby was so keyed up by the delay—the expectation of seeing her brother again, coupled with the fear that he would refuse to recognize her—that when she saw Mr. Byron she burst into shrieks of hysterical laughter: "That little man my brother! . . . perfectly ridiculous! . . . why, he looks just like a coachman! . . ." She shook like a jelly: "Oh Lord! Goodness me! . . . he's made a fool of your Mr. Pennington!"

"Please stop laughing, Mrs. Danby." Josephine's glance in my direction seemed to say 'if you're a man, get me out of this!' But Mrs. Danby didn't stop laughing, and I still felt powerless to intervene. In the dreadful silence that gradually fell on the Dive she pointed her finger at Mr. Byron and shouted: "I know who you are!"—she struggled with another fit of giggles—"yes, I know you, you're an impostor, a rotter. And, what's worse, your clothes don't fit you." When Mr.

Byron fixed his monocle into his eye and stared at her with cold dignity, he only started her off again.

"Who is that woman?" I heard him ask Moxon, and Moxon's reply was equally stagey: "Whoever she may be, she's certainly very ill-bred."

That remark was Moxon's undoing. Mrs. Danby, who had been wiping her glasses, put them on again and transferred her attention to him. She had stopped laughing abruptly, and now she said quite quietly to Josephine: "But I *do* know who *that* man is. He's the man that got my brother into that terrible trouble and allowed him to take all the blame."

"What's his name, Mrs. Danby?" asked Josephine, "quick, he's getting up to go. Tell me his name."

Mrs. Danby looked at her vacantly: "His name? I can't remember now. It was all so very long ago. . . . I thought for a moment it was *John Maningdon*."

CHAPTER FIFTEEN

Pandora's Box

(1)

"BUT MY DEAR SIR, it was only a lark, a harmless prank. You surely wouldn't be so harsh as to prosecute the poor fellow. . . . Picture the misery of an old actor once sought after by the Legitimate Stage, who has fallen to the degraded level of a potman in a Brixton public house! . . . For him, don't you see, it was a brief return to the stage of life, his final part, and one for which he rehearsed night and day, ever since I was ill-advised enough to tell him of his extraordinary resemblance to poor Milly. I admit I told him all I knew—yes, even down to the occasional stutter. But it never for a moment entered our heads that you would take our little escapade seriously!"

I said: "Mr. Moxon, it's hard to be in the position of the man who can't take a joke against himself. I'm prepared to believe that your old actor thought it was a lark. But I'm convinced you intended to get money out of us by false pretences, and I'm afraid the police will take the same view once they know of your intimate association with the man you once described as 'the greatest villain unhanged'."

"Sir!" Mr. Moxon had risen to his feet. "I don't like your insinuations."

"Oh, cut out the 'sir' and the 'dear sir'. I know you, Mr. Moxon—you're John Maningdon, late of the Jermyn blackmail case and the Travers murder case. You've always been good at keeping out of trouble. But now, if you don't want to end your days in prison, I want the truth, and the whole truth, about this attempt to cash in on a dead man's evil reputation."

Moxon sank back into his little box-like chair with his long arms hanging limply over the sides. He gave me a quick look and pulled up his trouser-legs almost to the knee, so that the glow of the gas-fire was reflected on his white, almost hairless shanks.

"So the old bitch *did* recognize me! Mrs. Kernan and I were pretty sure she had. That's why we did a bunk so hastily, leaving Byron to face the bill and the music." He held his nose for a moment between his forefinger and thumb, looking at me speculatively. Then his knees came together and he smacked them with the palms of his hands.

"Kennington, apart from being men of the world, you and I have something deeply in common. We both revere the memory of poor Milly. Would it interest you to know that it was all *his* idea from the beginning?"

"It would interest me profoundly, though I don't any longer feel bound to you by reverence for the memory of Milly. But, first of all, I want to get two things straight. Mrs. Danby is satisfied that the man who died as Percy Shelley in Marylebone Hospital couldn't possibly have been her brother, and I'm satisfied that Milly is dead or he wouldn't need an actor to impersonate him. What I want to know is when and where did he die, and what, if any, was his connection with Shelley?"

"His connection with Shelley? Why, they were as close as two hospital beds! Shelley was an old soldier of fortune, and Milly, as you said, was himself an old soldier. They got on like a house on fire, and after Shelley's death Milly never tired of talking about him—did I tell you the limerick?"

I nodded: "So your account of Milly in this house was partly based on his memories of Shelley? It was a composite character, and you and Mrs. Kernan evolved it between you so as to lead me via Somerset House to Marylebone? Why was Milly in Marylebone?"

"Cancer, as I told you, my dear . . . ahem, Kennington. You see, he had already been operated on a few years before. The operation was apparently successful, but eventually he had to go back to hospital—the cancer had turned up again in his marrow, and when they discovered that, they discharged him to die at home."

"At home?"

"Here, in this house in Brixton—it was the nearest to a home he had, under Mrs. Kernan's er . . . hospitable roof. He had known her well for some years and I believe he promised to leave her some money if she looked after him to the end."

I watched Moxon carefully as I said: "She had been Eddie Browne's mistress, hadn't she?—before Milly took her over?"

If I surprised him he showed no signs of it. "Eddie Browne? Ah, there's always another man, and I myself have been under her roof long enough to know that she's generous to a fault!"

I registered, and let it pass. "What name was he using when he died?"

"Percy Smith—you can confirm that easily."

"Did he know, when he was discharged from hospital, that he was condemned to die?"

"I think he did, but he wouldn't accept the sentence—he still had hopes of a *revival*. One day, a few weeks before he died, Mrs. Kernan showed him a newspaper account of a libel action in which a notorious devil-worshipper called Rookwood sued an authoress for libel. "Such stuff!" he said, and flung the paper away. "Why does nobody libel *me* nowadays?" Well, that thought became a sort of obsession, and most of his remaining time on earth was spent thinking out ways of doing a comeback. Only a few days before his death he said to me: 'John, what a lark it would be if I rose from the dead!' I said: 'What's the matter, Milly, are you getting religious?' He rambled on a bit, then he said: 'The vultures are circling over me, like they used to in old Shelley's stories . . . if only I could spoof them with another corpse, then get up behind and take a pot at them! . . . Shelley, you know, was just my age; it was his guts too that let him down in the end, and he hadn't any relations to worry about him . . .' That was all he said. He was too weak to think anything out."

"So after he was dead, you thought it out for him?"

"Put it that way if you like. But if you hadn't advertised in *The Times* I wouldn't have thought any more about it. As it was, I felt it my duty to carry out his dying wish. It was a stroke of ill-luck that you knew Mrs. Danby. I always understood from Milly that her husband had had her put away. Had she been, there was a sporting chance . . ."

Moxon sighed and brooded over the gas-fire, which was beginning to expire. At last he said: "Have you a shilling, Kennington? I'm damnably behind with my rent, and now Milly's dead I'm always afraid Mrs. Kernan may throw me out."

I found a shilling and the fire blazed up again. Moxon's spirits seemed to recover with it. "I've been frank with you, haven't I? Have you still the face to prosecute me?"

I said: "Mr. Moxon, you're a moral dinosaur. You really ought to be in a museum. Whether I prosecute you or not depends on the answer to one very personal question—did you know that Millington-Forsett was going to shoot Jack Travers?"

"No I didn't," he said promptly, "and by God nor did he! *It was a complete accident.*"

Despite Josephine's opinion, I *do* care for objective truth. But when Moxon said that, I felt as I had done when a boy at school assured me, on the authority of his free-thinking father, that the devil had no existence outside men's minds. I felt bitter.

"You're a liar!" I shouted. "He did mean to shoot him. Now I *shall* prosecute you."

"Go on then, and be damned! But it won't do you any good, because I shall write to the newspapers myself and expose the hollowness of your famous essay about the Travers murder."

We stared at each other in silence, neither prepared to give way. Moxon scraped his stubbly face with his hand and presently he said: "I'm a poor man. I could sell the truth to a newspaper, now Milly's in the news again. What's the story worth to you, Kennington? Shall we say fifty pounds?"

I said: "It may be worth nothing. I can't tell until I've heard it."

"All right, I shall assume that you're a man of honour. Well then, Milly never meant to shoot Travers, because Travers had been in the scheme from the beginning, though Jermyn didn't know it. The man he meant to kill was Jermyn, because he had threatened to tell Richmond if Milly didn't give up the whole idea. Jermyn was the traitor, and if Milly hadn't lost his bearings in the wood, trying to get his dog out of a rabbit-hole, he would have got what he deserved."

"But *you* knew Travers was in it?"

"For over forty years I never guessed. And I shouldn't know now if Milly hadn't confessed on his deathbed."

"*Confessed?*"

"Confessed that the only thing in life he had ever regretted was shooting Travers instead of Jermyn!"

(2)

As soon as I had verified Moxon's statement, I began the first draft of this book, working at top speed. I wanted to see the dossier it was based on safely deposited with Hodge and

Ricketts, so that if Eddie's threats were ever put into effect my notes could be handed to the police.

I had foreseen that the publication of *A Twist Somewhere* would be the signal for the vultures to start picking at Milly, but I hadn't realized that there would be so many, and it hadn't occurred to me that the revival of interest in the Travers case would excite editors to organize a posthumous manhunt. I told myself that I held all the trumps and that if I kept quiet the others would soon have nothing to say. When editors asked me for articles, I turned them down flatly on the grounds that I was writing a book. But there again I miscalculated.

A Sunday newspaper, exasperated by my reticence, rang up Hodge and Ricketts. Ricketts confirmed that I was writing a book, but added darkly that it might be years before it could be published since it contained revelations which for private reasons could not yet be made public. That set the editor guessing, and having worked up his readers' interest, he was in no mood to let the subject drop. He put his entire Crime Bureau on the trail and started pestering everybody from Josephine's parents to Mrs. Danby.

One Sunday morning not long after the cocktail party Josephine and I were wandering by the Serpentine, enjoying the first sunshine for a week. We stopped to watch a child feeding gulls from a bag. As he threw up the bread, the wheeling gulls came screeching in with claws outstretched and wings braking, and their shadows swirled about our feet. We stood there mesmerized by all that whiteness and movement. Then Josephine's arm tightened on mine.

"When two people feel as we do, there's no reason to be afraid, is there?"

I said: "What on earth are you talking about?"

"Oh, nothing, really. Did you see the review in this

morning's *Sunday Mail*, headed *Pandora's Box*? Your book is described as a fascinating crime titbit, a foretaste of the banquet Raymond Kennington will shortly put before his readers."

"Well?"

"That's what I'm wondering. What will Eddie and Co. think of it?"

The very next day there was an awkward article in the *Mirror*, by a retired C.I.D. detective who had worked with the Eire police on the enquiry into the Career Girls' Bureau. Millington-Forsett, he asserted, had been the spider at the centre of an international organization, in which 'hundreds of innocent girls were destroyed'. His conclusion was: 'Millington-Forsett and his aides slipped through our fingers, to continue the evil traffic elsewhere. Though the chief is dead, his friends will do well to remember that the arm of the Yard is as long as its memory, and its patience is inexhaustible.'

Eddie had said: 'If you miscue, you'll feel hot breath down your neck, like a hunted character in one of your books.' I hadn't 'miscued', yet I was already beginning to turn round in the street, to jump when a car backfired, to make a rule of taking taxis home at night. I now saw why Josephine thought Pimlico sinister. . . .

All this hastened on our marriage and increased my consumption of alcohol. When I awoke one afternoon to find the Abyss yawning beneath me, it took Josephine some time to convince me that I was over the French Alps, married to her, drunk on champagne and flying south on my honeymoon.

It was our first escape from circumstances, and in a day or two of being able to concentrate on ourselves, we became Josephine and Raymond unequivocally. We became relaxed and vegetable in the high autumn of Mediterranean December ripe with oranges and lemons and with golden leaves that still clung to the deciduous trees. We insured against time and fate by doing our best to beget a child, who would be called Josephina Raye.

We came back to a furnished flat in Chelsea ready to face anything. Though we had kept our marriage as dark as we could, our engagement had already been publicly announced, and there had been a number of journalists outside the Registrar's Office. As a result of that renewed publicity we collected quite a lot of wedding presents, of which at least a dozen were from my 'public'. I had two pipes from quite separate ladies who had seen my photograph on the back of *A Twist Somewhere* and thought I might need comforting in my marriage; and I had a pewter beer-mug from a cynic called H. de Seuta in Broadstairs, who asked me if I were aware that 'malt can do more than Memsahibs can to glorify the wondrous works of Pan!'

On our first night in our temporary home we amused ourselves by going through the accumulation of letters and parcels. Near the bottom of my pile of letters I came on one addressed in childish handwriting to Raymond Kennington, Esquire, Care of Hodge and Ricketts. Inside was a sheet of white notepaper on which was gummed a black, composite, newspaper headline: TERRIBLE ACCIDENT. AUTHOR AND BRIDE DIE IN AGONY.

I looked at Josephine. Then I put it in my pocket without saying a word. If, as seemed likely, Josephina Raye was a *fait accompli*, I wanted her to have a good start . . .

Next morning, when Josephine went back to work, I made my way deviously to Scotland Yard and managed, after a considerable wait, to steal an hour of Bairstow's time. Having lectured me about the folly of 'crime amateurs' getting themselves involved in the underworld, he was prepared to listen attentively while I told him what had happened in Paris. When I had finished I handed him my anonymous letter and asked him what he thought I ought to do about it.

"H'm," he said, holding the letter up to the light, "I suppose you're assuming some connection between this letter and your friend Eddie Browne?"

"I should have thought that was obvious."

"Obvious?—we don't like that word in our profession. You know, I don't want to discourage you, but there are people in this country who collect this sort of letter—that's the price of fame, you know!"

"You mean I oughtn't to take it seriously?"

"I didn't say that. What I do say is, don't over-estimate it. If this gang were really out for your blood, would they be likely to tell you so? Of course, we can't rule out the possibility that they are concerned about certain articles in the Press and want to remind you to watch your step. But on the face of it this letter looks to me like the work of one of those harmless idiots with a grudge against society. They work the poison out of their systems by putting the wind up complete strangers. . . ." He paused, whistling through his teeth as he tapped them with a pencil: "I'll tell you what we'll do, we'll get our experts on the job right away. Meanwhile, keep in touch with us and let us know at once if you get any more of these *billy doos*. . . . By the way, I haven't got your new address and phone number. . . ."

I had been patronized, contradicted, treated as an amateur and a fool—and all, I told myself, because Bairstow was jealous of me! But after a drink or two I began to see the point of his deflating technique. Being made to feel smaller did somehow make me feel less vulnerable.

I wasn't going to take any risks, however, especially where Josephine was concerned. For the next few days I went to fetch her from the office at lunchtime and I was there to pick her up every night. Josephine thought it all very odd.

"Darling," she said, "you can't keep this up. Our honeymoon's over and this is marriage . . . what on earth's happened to that self-centred, reluctant bachelor?"

"He died of a broken ego. Didn't Ricketts say that bachelors always fall like a ton of bricks? Anyway, you need looking after just now: when Josephina's born, *she* can look after you."

It was impossible to keep an eye on her all the time without making her suspicious. Fortunately there was Betty, the telephone girl at Hodge and Ricketts, who had always been an ally of mine. When I told her over a secret drink that one of Josephine's old followers was making a nuisance of himself, she became all complicity at once: she had always thought of Josephine as fast, as having more men than her 'position' warranted. Now she agreed never to let Josephine go out without finding some excuse to ask her where she was going.

It was Betty who rang up breathlessly one afternoon to tell me that Josephine had gone out for tea at the Fleet Bunshop: there had been a man hanging about outside the office all day and she had seen him go after Josephine.

I asked her to describe him, then I rang for a taxi and dashed for the Fleet Bunshop, arriving just as Josephine was getting up to go.

"Raymond! Is anything wrong?"

I had picked her out at once, but I had looked right through her at the only man in that roomful of women. He was at the back of the café, behind her, his face hidden by the *Evening News*. He had thin reddish hair and wore a Burberry, which agreed with Betty's description.

"I had to go down to Cornhill about those investments and I called in at the office on the way back. . . . Betty told me you'd gone out for tea, so I, well, I just thought I'd join you."

"But I've had tea—I must be getting back."

I sat down firmly in the seat opposite her, which gave me a good view of the red-haired man, and Josephine sat down again, saying: "You look as though you need a whiskey. Has something happened to Josephina's nest-egg?"

"Nothing serious, but all this talk of war isn't good for Housing Estates. I've told Barber to sell at a slight loss and buy Consolidated Nickels."

Josephine looked reassured, and I said: "How's life in the office today?"

"Steady. Hodge's cold has sunk to his tubes and the Pest rang up again."

The Pest was Mrs. Danby. Ever since the great Millington-Forsett hoax she had been ringing up Josephine for chats about cats: she seemed to have taken a great fancy to her.

"Does she still think you're the vet's wife?"

"No, she's lucid for the moment. She's read that you're going to publish another book about her brother and that seems to have upset her—she thinks she can tell you things about Milly that will make you change your attitude. . . ."

The red-haired man put down his paper and beckoned to the waitress. As I took in the little moustache, the slightly hollow cheeks and the mouth that seemed too full of teeth, I had an unpleasant shock of recognition. Had I really seen that face before, or was it one of those type-faces familiarized by some well-known film star? Then he spoke to the waitress, protruding his lower lip, and the picture jumped into context. I had seen him in our pub in Chelsea, one of a group I had assumed to be locals. I had noticed him particularly because of his way of playing darts, lower lip protruding, little finger sticking out in self-conscious technical refinement. . . .

Josephine was saying: "She wants you to come and see her urgently, if possible this evening. . . . Raymond, you're not listening!"

I started guiltily and stopped staring at the red-haired man.

"Of course I'm listening. Mrs. D. wants me to come and see her, but wild horses wouldn't drag me into her flat again."

"Then I'll go," Josephine said stubbornly, "that's a stone we can't afford to leave unturned."

I took Josephine back to the office and then I crossed the road to a telephone box in a quiet alley leading to Lincoln's Inn Fields. I had decided to ring up Bairstow and tell him we were being followed. I was in such a hurry that I had my hand on the handle of the telephone box door before I realized it was occupied.

It was occupied by the red-haired man.

He was too absorbed to notice me and I stood there for a full minute wondering what I was going to do. Evidently he was having difficulty in getting through. He kept putting pennies in the box and then pressing Button B to get them back. I was used to telephoning from call-boxes in crowded parts of London and I had so often been kept waiting, watching the pantomime in the glass box in an agony of impatience, that by the time he started speaking into the instrument, I knew that he had had to dial Operator and get through that way.

That gave me an idea. I walked quickly away into the shadow of a Gothic archway and waited there till I saw him emerge from the telephone box. When he had disappeared in the direction of the Strand I went into the call-box and dialled O. I said: "This is Detective-Inspector Bairstow of Scotland Yard—I want you to give me the number of the last call from the box." The girl said: "Wait a moment please", then, "I'm sorry, Sir, it's against regulations, you'll have to send round to the Exchange." I said: "This is a matter of life and death. If I don't get the number you'll have reason to be sorry." I held my breath while she whispered to somebody. Then she said: "The last call from this box was to New Scotland Yard—surely I needn't tell *you* the number!"

CHAPTER SIXTEEN

"Oh, my beloved pussies!"

So BAIRSTOW had taken the letter seriously. For a moment I didn't know whether to be alarmed at having my sense of danger confirmed, or to feel safer in the knowledge that the police were watching over us. Finally I had to face it— Scotland Yard was a great comfort.

Before I left the call-box I rang Mrs. Danby and arranged to come round and see her after dinner.

My previous visit to Gladstone Road was still the vividest of my unpleasant memories and in view of all the pain my book must have caused Mrs. Danby I don't think I would have dared go again if I hadn't had Josephine to act as a psychological buffer. I heartily agreed when she suggested that it would be a delicate attention to take some buns and liver for Mrs. Danby's cats. But since the cats themselves were part of the ordeal I insisted on Josephine drenching herself in scent, while I went armed with a packet of *Gauloises*, saved from our honeymoon. That was to have important consequences.

On the telephone Mrs. Danby had been lucid, if ominously polite. Now, as she opened the door to us, I had the impression that she was crazier than ever.

"How nice of you to come, Mrs. Pennington," she said, extending a grubby hand with the swooping grace of an Edwardian hostess. Then, as we followed her into the sitting-room: "I think you know all my family?"

Josephine rose to the occasion. Bowing right and left, she said: "I've heard so much about them from my husband— I've brought along a little present."

Mrs. Danby opened the bag and pounced on the liver

greedily. "Oh my dear," she said, "oh my *dear*, how extremely thoughtful and kind of you!"

Suddenly she seemed to notice me. "But you, Mr. Kennington with a K, *you* don't like my family, do you?"

Josephine reminded me with a glance not to let myself be put in the wrong. I took my cue and said: "Mrs. Danby, I told you, when we first met, that my view of your brother was based on the available evidence, that if you could tell me anything to make me change that view I would consider myself bound to make amends publicly. I've come here, don't forget, at *your* request, on the understanding that you have something urgent to tell me about your brother."

That seemed to impress her. She looked at me vaguely and said: "Yes, yes, I have letters of Nevil's that you ought to see. Sit down, please, both of you, and do smoke as much as you want, while I go and look them out."

She disappeared into the bedroom, shutting the door behind her, while Josephine and I puffed away apprehensively. I pointed to the photograph of Millington-Forsett and his sister on the mantelpiece. Josephine studied it for a moment, nodding as she recognized her own mental image.

Presently Mrs. Danby reappeared and beckoned us into the bedroom. It was a small room, hot and stuffy from the fumes of an oil-stove. In one corner was a litter of torn-up newspapers, hastily pushed there with carpet sweepings and paper bags as though she had been turning out her flat on the eve of departure. Here and there round the walls were tattered cushions and odd garments which obviously served as beds for the cats. Crumbs and food-fragments clogged the cracks between the varnished planks of the flooring.

But it was the bed we chiefly noticed. It had not been made, and the rumpled sheets were strewn with letters, some of them yellow with age.

"There you are!" Mrs. Danby pointed at the bed triumphantly: "There are all the letters my brother ever wrote me. When you have read through them you will know what sort of a man Nevil really was—kind, generous and affectionate. . . ."

"But Mrs. Danby," I said, momentarily bewildered, " I can't read through all those letters now. If you will allow me to take them away with me . . .?"

"Certainly not. These letters shall never leave my house— they are all you have left me of my brother."

"But Mrs. Danby, I promise . . ."

"I don't trust you, Mr. Kennington. Since you published your infamous book, I have been insulted almost daily by reporters ringing me up or trying to worm their way into my flat. Only yesterday a man came in here pretending he was from the Gas Company . . . he wanted to pry, to take photographs . . . but we sent him packing, didn't we, pussies?"

In that macabre setting, by the light of a naked bulb, Josephine and I knelt by the bed and started looking through the letters. . . .

At first it seemed hopeless trying to read them with Mrs. Danby standing over us, sucking peppermints with odd spasmodic movements of her jaw, but gradually I succumbed to their fascination and I forgot about Mrs. Danby. For weeks I had been fitting together the skeleton of Millington-Forsett: but these letters were like dried fragments of his flesh, the sensitive envelope of the man.

Maggie [I read, in a letter dated 1916 from a hotel in Roehampton]—Maggie, you little rascal foolbones, can't you touch that husband of yours once more? If you do, I promise I'll never ask again. Surely, *surely*, he wouldn't

notice a hundred quid—especially if you sent it c/o
Corporal C. Dixon at the Roehampton Hospital for Dis-
abled Soldiers? You know perfectly well you'll get it back,
and with whopping interest . . .

Another letter, which Josephine handed me without comment, was dated 1929 from Greshams, Dublin:

> Maggieshins, I'm in the money at last and thinking of
> buying you a nice, quiet little place in the country, with a
> nurse to look after you and a good leech handy. Now that
> you're so much better there can be no question whatever
> of your going back to that terrible place near Margate.
> Of course you're not mad. What an idea! You wait until
> I catch another doctor saying it. But I do think you need
> rest and proper care—*cancer* isn't a thing to neglect. . . .

The combined stench of Josephine's scent, my Gauloise
and the oil-stove, was so overpowering that the odour of
paraffin only came to me gradually, as a new irritant to the
mucous membranes.

I didn't look up until Mrs. Danby had almost finished
sprinkling the threadbare carpet. She was doing it methodi-
cally, almost tenderly, like a gardener watering the seedlings.
But when I shouted: "Mrs. Danby, what are you doing?" she
acted with the speed and agility of a young woman. Before I
could stop her, she had kicked over the oil-stove and was
already retreating to the doorway, a squat black figure with
a mop of grey hair, calling urgently to the two cats who had
been rubbing round our legs while we read the letters. By the
time I had caught Josephine's arm and got her to the door,
Mrs. Danby had locked it on the other side, and as I vainly
flung my shoulder against it, her sharp appeal to the cats had
sunk to a low, hysterical wail: "Pussies, oh my beloved
pussies!"

We turned round to see the sheet of flame from the over-turned stove running along the carpet towards the bed. There was a screech from the cats and suddenly one of them was halfway up the wall clawing at the wallpaper in its panic, every hair erect and staring: the other, with all four paws hooked into the curtains, hung there hissing, nerves and muscles galvanized by the terrible voltage of animal terror.

"Mrs. Danby," I pleaded, banging on the door, "Mrs. Danby, let us out. You can't mean to burn us alive."

The answer from the other side was the demonic wailing of the mad woman: "Burn, burn, you cad! Burn, you happy young married pair! Burn, burn, as you are making poor Nevil burn in hell! Burn for me and my ruined family!"

Josephine said: "Quick, the window! If the drop isn't too long we might be able to knot the sheets together." But as I flung open the windows and looked down, Josephine was driven back from the bed. The draught had caught the fire under it, and in a moment the whole thing was a mass of flame, the letters of Millington-Forsett withering into black flakes that swirled up in the hot air-current and winged past me on the rush of fumes and smoke. . . . At that moment the lights went out and I felt a sharp pain on my cheek and neck. I leant out shouting: "Fire! Help!" and the pain on my neck was so excruciating that I thought for a moment the curtain had caught fire behind me. But as I snatched with one hand over my shoulder I grasped what felt like fur stretched over steel. I plucked the desperate cat off me and flung it screaming out of the window. . . .

There was no light now but the flickering of the flames, no sound but the wails of Mrs. Danby above the hiss and crackle of her obscene possessions being destroyed. We tried to tear the curtains down, but after a moment's struggle gave it up. They were too thick to knot successfully, too flimsy to be used for smothering the flames. Our only hope was to get out.

We looked down into the courtyard formed by the tall blocks of flats and all round us windows were being opened, lights springing up. There was a babel of voices yelling advice and I remember a man at the window directly opposite and just above us leaning out in his pyjamas, shouting: "Hang on, the firemen are on the way. If it gets too hot, climb out of the window and stand on the cornice—we'll get sheets to catch you if you fall."

I looked down at the square of concrete forty feet below and my head swam. Then it cleared again and through streaming tears I saw the cornice, a shadow projecting from the brickwork. I also saw the iron staircase outside Mrs. Danby's kitchen window. It couldn't have been more than twenty feet away, separated from us by the outside wall of her sitting-room. A man ran across the courtyard with a length of rope and started clattering up the iron staircase in what sounded like hobnail boots. He was barely halfway up when I decided that we would have to get out.

Josephine made a sound that was half choke and half sob as I caught her in my arms and lifted her up on to the window-sill. She was perfectly calm, despite the trembling, and as she sat there for a moment, resting, she said softly: "Goodbye, Raymond, goodbye, darling—we did have fun."

"Goodbye nothing!" I said fiercely. "We're going to get through this. Now do exactly as I tell you."

She clasped her arms round my neck and let herself slide down the wall. "Now you've got to get out," she panted, as soon as she felt her feet touch the cornice. "I'm all right now —I can hang on to the window-sill."

Far below there were men with lights and a sheet. By the lights of the flat overlooking us I saw that the man with the rope had reached the top of the spiral staircase. He was standing on the small iron landing outside Mrs. Danby's kitchen. He had been battering vainly on the door. Now he was telling me: "Catch the rope and make it fast to the drainpipe. I've attached it here. You can cross the gap walking on the cornice. But whatever you do, don't look down."

By this time the heat behind me was so intense that I had to leave Josephine to hang on by herself and climb out astraddle the window-sill.

There was a confusion of contradictory advice, which seemed to be coming from all sides. But I was tuned in to the man on the fire-escape. He was of our world: I could talk to him almost intimately.

I leant out as far as I could with one arm outstretched, and as the rope struck my wrist I grabbed at it. I was conscious of a great groan rising up, then the voice said calmly: "Okay, next time lucky. Watch it, take your time and you can't miss."

It came again and this time I caught it. But the space between the drainpipe and the wall was too narrow for the thickness of the rope. I struggled for what seemed an age before I got it through, stabbing at it with a silver pencil.

When I had made it fast I said: "Go on, darling, you're first. I'll come right after you. Trust the rope and don't look down."

Josephine nodded, looked at me for a second full in the eyes, then edged away face to the wall, arms outstretched along the rope.

As I watched her take the first hesitant steps, falter, sway out against the taut rope, and then back against the wall, I felt infinitely remote from my own body. I was so much with her, every inch of that dreadful crossing, that I hardly felt the pain in my leg as the boards under the window started to flame. The thumping of my heart might have been somebody else trying to hammer down a door with his fists. And my voice, as I tried to shout at the white faces below: "Watch that drainpipe doesn't give", was like the unnatural muttering of a ventriloquist's dummy.

Josephine had reached Mrs. Danby's sitting-room window when a searchlight was suddenly switched on from below and she was printed across the brickwork like a huge black crucifixion. I hadn't heard the ringing of the firebell. I had been completely unconscious of the commotion below as the fire-engine drew up and the turn-table ladder started to extend to the whirring of lowgeared power. Now I saw the lengths of steel rising up one out of the other, and the man with the brass helmet, hooked on to a tiny platform, swaying in a great arc of shadow.

"Oh God," I heard my own voice praying, "make him come quicker. She can't hold out for more than a few seconds."

Suddenly I could see Josephine's face distinctly. It was very white, her eyes were half closed and her lips were moving. For a moment I wondered where the light was coming from. Then I remembered Mrs. Danby. She had drawn the curtains of her sitting-room. A second later I heard the window slam up and Mrs. Danby's head came through the window, transfigured into a Medusa.

There was no sound in the world now but the whirring of machinery and an old, strident voice, sawing away at Josephine's failing consciousness. "You shan't escape me, Mrs. Kennington—I've caught you and you're going to DIE." There was a peal of hysterical laughter and a flash of light stabbed me in the eye. Mrs. Danby had a long carving knife. She was hacking at Josephine, who clung to the rope with one hand and tried to ward off the blows with the other. . . .

Then the miracle happened. A jet of water hit Mrs. Danby full in the face, so that her whole head seemed to explode into dazzling liquefaction, leaving the window blessedly empty.

A second later strong arms, rising out of the shadow, caught Josephine round the waist. . . .

The room was dark, and the pain in my head and legs didn't worry me. It was remote, somehow, on the other side of a dark hedge of cypress. I didn't know where I was till I heard Bairstow saying: "All right, Sister. But as soon as he's properly round I want to have a talk with him."

I tried to sit up and gave a moan: "Josephine—where's Josephine?"

"Mrs. Kennington is in another ward of this hospital"—it was the Sister who spoke. The voice was kind and impersonal, and I could almost hear the creaking of the starched uniform: "She's got a few superficial wounds on the arms and she's suffering from bad nervous shock, but she's going to be as right as rain. Now don't worry any more. Just be a good boy and lie still. You're the one we're worried about—you've got concussion and a badly burnt leg."

Bairstow said: "You're in Coventry, old man. You're lucky not to find yourself in gaol for provoking a serious breach of the peace!"

I said: "Oh!" I could just make out his shadowy figure, but my eyes wouldn't focus properly. I felt like a herring smoked alive and there was some sort of erection over my leg. Gradually it all came back to me—I remembered fainting on the window-sill and I deduced that I must have fallen back into Mrs. Danby's bedroom.

"Mrs. Danby—what happened to her?"

"Oh, don't you worry about her. She's detained at His

Majesty's pleasure, and likely to be for the rest of her natural life."

A door banged somewhere along the corridor and I felt a wave of hot gooseflesh passing up my leg, succeeded by an agonizing sequence of involuntary muscular twitches. The Sister said: "Now, Detective Inspector, that's enough—I told you he wasn't well enough."

I said: "Please don't go for a minute. I can't rest until I know one more thing—did Mrs. Danby write that letter?"

"Of course she did. I never thought for a moment it had been written by the people you were afraid of, and as soon as you left me I was able to confirm it from one of my colleagues. A month before that, Interpol had been on to us for information about Eddie Browne. Apparently he came to a sticky end, shot down by his own gang in the middle of Paris in broad daylight. Before he died he broke the Underworld law of silence and gave the French police the chance they'd been waiting for for years. They've got Mattei and his boys and I reckon the information you've collected is going to interest them quite a lot, as corroborating Eddie Browne's statement. . . ."

I said: "Poor bastard!—excuse me, Sister."

Bairstow said: "*Bastard* is right. We've found out that Eddie Browne was a son of Jermyn, the blackmailer in the Travers case. Turning King's Evidence seems to have run in the family; that's presumably why Millington-Forsett was so keen to get him involved in the Twight murder. Jermyn was dead, so he bided his time—forty-six years—and revenged himself on Jermyn's son. . . ."

Bairstow droned on, but I was no longer listening.

Under my scorched eyelids I saw flames and a raucous voice was wailing deep in my consciousness: "Burn, you cad!

Burn for my ruined family! Burn, as you've made poor Nevil burn in hell! . . ."

Then I felt the prick of a needle and the Sister swears she heard me muttering: "Blessed be the God of Shadrach, Meshach and Abed-Nego!"

THE PERENNIAL LIBRARY MYSTERY SERIES

Delano Ames

FOR OLD CRIME'S SAKE (*available 12/82*)　　　P 629, $2.84

MURDER, MAESTRO, PLEASE (*available 12/82*)　　P 630, $2.84
"If there is a more engaging couple in modern fiction than Jane and
Dagobert Brown, we have not met them."　　　　　　　*—Scotsman*

E. C. Bentley

TRENT'S LAST CASE　　　　　　　　　　　　　　P 440, $2.50
"One of the three best detective stories ever written."
　　　　　　　　　　　　　　　　　　　　　　—Agatha Christie

TRENT'S OWN CASE　　　　　　　　　　　　　　P 516, $2.25
"I won't waste time saying that the plot is sound and the detection
satisfying. Trent has not altered a scrap and reappears with all his old
humor and charm."　　　　　　　　　　　　　*—Dorothy L. Sayers*

Gavin Black

A DRAGON FOR CHRISTMAS　　　　　　　　　　P 473, $1.95
"Potent excitement!"　　　　　　　　*—New York Herald Tribune*

THE EYES AROUND ME　　　　　　　　　　　　P 485, $1.95
"I stayed up until all hours last night reading *The Eyes Around Me,*
which is something I do not do very often, but I was so intrigued by the
ingeniousness of Mr. Black's plotting and the witty way in which he spins
his mystery. I can only say that I enjoyed the book enormously."
　　　　　　　　　　　　　　　　　　　　—F. van Wyck Mason

YOU WANT TO DIE, JOHNNY?　　　　　　　　　P 472, $1.95
"Gavin Black doesn't just develop a pressure plot in suspense, he adds
uninfected wit, character, charm, and sharp knowledge of the Far East
to make rereading as keen as the first race-through."　　*—Book Week*

Nicholas Blake

THE CORPSE IN THE SNOWMAN　　　　　　　　P 427, $1.95
"If there is a distinction between the novel and the detective story (which
we do not admit), then this book deserves a high place in both catego-
ries."　　　　　　　　　　　　　　　　　　*—The New York Times*

THE DREADFUL HOLLOW   P 493, $1.95
"Pace unhurried, characters excellent, reasoning solid."
— *San Francisco Chronicle*

END OF CHAPTER   P 397, $1.95
". . . admirably solid . . . an adroit formal detective puzzle backed up by firm characterization and a knowing picture of London publishing."
— *The New York Times*

HEAD OF A TRAVELER   P 398, $2.25
"Another grade A detective story of the right old jigsaw persuasion."
— *New York Herald Tribune Book Review*

MINUTE FOR MURDER   P 419, $1.95
"An outstanding mystery novel. Mr. Blake's writing is a delight in itself."
— *The New York Times*

THE MORNING AFTER DEATH   P 520, $1.95
"One of Blake's best."
— Rex Warner

A PENKNIFE IN MY HEART   P 521, $2.25
"Style brilliant . . . and suspenseful."   — *San Francisco Chronicle*

THE PRIVATE WOUND   P 531, $2.25
"[Blake's] best novel in a dozen years . . . . An intensely penetrating study of sexual passion . . . . A powerful story of murder and its aftermath."
— Anthony Boucher, *The New York Times*

A QUESTION OF PROOF   P 494, $1.95
"The characters in this story are unusually well drawn, and the suspense is well sustained."
— *The New York Times*

THE SAD VARIETY   P 495, $2.25
"It is a stunner. I read it instead of eating, instead of sleeping."
— Dorothy Salisbury Davis

THERE'S TROUBLE BREWING   P 569, $3.37
"Nigel Strangeways is a puzzling mixture of simplicity and penetration, but all the more real for that."   — *The Times Literary Supplement*

THOU SHELL OF DEATH   P 428, $1.95
"It has all the virtues of culture, intelligence and sensibility that the most exacting connoisseur could ask of detective fiction."
— *The Times Literary Supplement*

Nicholas Blake (cont'd)

THE WHISPER IN THE GLOOM   P 418, $1.95
"One of the most entertaining suspense-pursuit novels in many seasons."
— *The New York Times*

THE WIDOW'S CRUISE   P 399, $2.25
"A stirring suspense. . . . The thrilling tale leaves nothing to be desired."
— *Springfield Republican*

THE WORM OF DEATH   P 400, $2.25
"It [The Worm of Death] is one of Blake's very best—and his best is better than almost anyone's."
— Louis Untermeyer

John & Emery Bonett

A BANNER FOR PEGASUS   P 554, $2.40
"A gem! Beautifully plotted and set. . . . Not only is the murder adroit and deserved, and the detection competent, but the love story is charming."
— Jacques Barzun and Wendell Hertig Taylor

DEAD LION   P 563, $2.40
"A clever plot, authentic background and interesting characters highly recommended this one."
— *New Republic*

Christianna Brand

GREEN FOR DANGER   P 551, $2.50
"You have to reach for the greatest of Great Names (Christie, Carr, Queen . . .) to find Brand's rivals in the devious subtleties of the trade."
— Anthony Boucher

TOUR DE FORCE   P 572, $2.40
"Complete with traps for the over-ingenious, a double-reverse surprise ending and a key clue planted so fairly and obviously that you completely overlook it. If that's your idea of perfect entertainment, then seize at once upon *Tour de Force.*"
— Anthony Boucher, *The New York Times*

James Byrom

OR BE HE DEAD   P 585, $2.84
"A very original tale . . . Well written and steadily entertaining."
— Jacques Barzun & Wendell Hertig Taylor, *A Catalogue of Crime*

Marjorie Carleton

VANISHED P 559, $2.40
"Exceptional . . . a minor triumph."
—Jacques Barzun and Wendell Hertig Taylor, *A Catalogue of Crime*

George Harmon Coxe

MURDER WITH PICTURES P 527, $2.25
"[Coxe] has hit the bull's-eye with his first shot."
—*The New York Times*

Edmund Crispin

BURIED FOR PLEASURE P 506, $2.50
"Absolute and unalloyed delight."
—Anthony Boucher, *The New York Times*

Lionel Davidson

THE MENORAH MEN (*available 10/82*) P 592, $2.84
"Of his fellow thriller writers, only John Le Carré shows the same instinct for the viscera." —*Chicago Tribune*

THE NIGHT OF WENCESLAS (*available 10/82*) P 595, $2.84
"A most ingenious thriller, so enriched with style, wit, and a sense of serious comedy that it all but transcends its kind."
—*The New Yorker*

THE ROSE OF TIBET (*available 10/82*) P 593, $2.84
"I hadn't realized how much I missed the genuine Adventure story . . . until I read *The Rose of Tibet*." —Graham Greene

D. M. Devine

MY BROTHER'S KILLER P 558, $2.40
"A most enjoyable crime story which I enjoyed reading down to the last moment." —Agatha Christie

Kenneth Fearing

THE BIG CLOCK P 500, $1.95
"It will be some time before chill-hungry clients meet again so rare a compound of irony, satire, and icy-fingered narrative. *The Big Clock* is . . . a psychothriller you won't put down." —*Weekly Book Review*

Andrew Garve

THE ASHES OF LODA   P 430, $1.50
"Garve . . . embellishes a fine fast adventure story with a more credible
picture of the U.S.S.R. than is offered in most thrillers."
                                        —*The New York Times Book Review*

THE CUCKOO LINE AFFAIR   P 451, $1.95
". . . an agreeable and ingenious piece of work."   —*The New Yorker*

A HERO FOR LEANDA   P 429, $1.50
"One can trust Mr. Garve to put a fresh twist to any situation, and the
ending is really a lovely surprise."   —*The Manchester Guardian*

MURDER THROUGH THE LOOKING GLASS   P 449, $1.95
". . . refreshingly out-of-the-way and enjoyable . . . highly recommended
to all comers."   —*Saturday Review*

NO TEARS FOR HILDA   P 441, $1.95
"It starts fine and finishes finer. I got behind on breathing watching Max
get not only his man but his woman, too."   —Rex Stout

THE RIDDLE OF SAMSON   P 450, $1.95
"The story is an excellent one, the people are quite likable, and the
writing is superior."   —*Springfield Republican*

Michael Gilbert

BLOOD AND JUDGMENT   P 446, $1.95
"Gilbert readers need scarcely be told that the characters all come alive
at first sight, and that his surpassing talent for narration enhances any
plot. . . . Don't miss."   —*San Francisco Chronicle*

THE BODY OF A GIRL   P 459, $1.95
"Does what a good mystery should do: open up into all kinds of ramifica-
tions, with untold menace behind the action. At the end, there is a
bang-up climax, and it is a pleasure to see how skilfully Gilbert wraps
everything up."   —*The New York Times Book Review*

THE DANGER WITHIN   P 448, $1.95
"Michael Gilbert has nicely combined some elements of the straight
detective story with plenty of action, suspense, and adventure, to produce a superior thriller."   —*Saturday Review*

FEAR TO TREAD   P 458, $1.95
"Merits serious consideration as a work of art."
                                                    —*The New York Times*

C. W. Grafton

BEYOND A REASONABLE DOUBT   P 519, $1.95
"A very ingenious tale of murder . . . a brilliant and gripping narrative."
                              —Jacques Barzun and Wendell Hertig Taylor

Edward Grierson

THE SECOND MAN   P 528, $2.25
"One of the best trial-testimony books to have come along in quite a
while."   —*The New Yorker*

Cyril Hare

DEATH IS NO SPORTSMAN   P 555, $2.40
"You will be thrilled because it succeeds in placing an ingenious story
in a new and refreshing setting. . . . The identity of the murderer is really
a surprise."   —*Daily Mirror*

DEATH WALKS THE WOODS   P 556, $2.40
"Here is a fine formal detective story, with a technically brilliant solution
demanding the attention of all connoisseurs of construction."
                              —Anthony Boucher, *The New York Times Book Review*

AN ENGLISH MURDER   P 455, $2.50
"By a long shot, the best crime story I have read for a long time.
Everything is traditional, but originality does not suffer. The setting is
perfect. Full marks to Mr. Hare."   —*Irish Press*

TENANT FOR DEATH   P 570, $2.84
"The way in which an air of probability is combined both with clear,
terse narrative and with a good deal of subtle suburban atmosphere,
proves the extreme skill of the writer."   —*The Spectator*

TRAGEDY AT LAW   P 522, $2.25
"An extremely urbane and well-written detective story."
                                                —*The New York Times*

UNTIMELY DEATH   P 514, $2.25
"The English detective story at its quiet best, meticulously underplayed,
rich in perceivings of the droll human animal and ready at the last with
a neat surprise which has been there all the while had we but wits to see
it."   —*New York Herald Tribune Book Review*

THE WIND BLOWS DEATH   P 589, $2.84
"A plot compounded of musical knowledge, a Dickens allusion, and a
subtle point in law is related with delightfully unobtrusive wit, warmth,
and style."   —*The New York Times*

Cyril Hare (cont'd)

WITH A BARE BODKIN   P 523, $2.25
"One of the best detective stories published for a long time."
           —*The Spectator*

Robert Harling

THE ENORMOUS SHADOW   P 545, $2.50
"In some ways the best spy story of the modern period. . . . The writing
is terse and vivid . . . the ending full of action . . . altogether first-rate."
—Jacques Barzun and Wendell Hertig Taylor, *A Catalogue of Crime*

Matthew Head

THE CABINDA AFFAIR   P 541, $2.25
"An absorbing whodunit and a distinguished novel of atmosphere."
       —Anthony Boucher, *The New York Times*

THE CONGO VENUS (*available 11/82*)   P 597, $2.84
"Terrific. The dialogue is just plain wonderful."
           —*The Boston Globe*

MURDER AT THE FLEA CLUB   P 542, $2.50
"The true delight is in Head's style, its limpid ease combined with humor
and an awesome precision of phrase."   —*San Francisco Chronicle*

M. V. Heberden

ENGAGED TO MURDER   P 533, $2.25
"Smooth plotting."   —*The New York Times*

James Hilton

WAS IT MURDER?   P 501, $1.95
"The story is well planned and well written."
           —*The New York Times*

P. M. Hubbard

HIGH TIDE   P 571, $2.40
"A smooth elaboration of mounting horror and danger."
           —*Library Journal*

Elspeth Huxley

THE AFRICAN POISON MURDERS   P 540, $2.25
"Obscure venom, maniacal mutilations, deadly bush fire, thrilling climax compose major opus.... Top-flight."
—Saturday Review of Literature

MURDER ON SAFARI (*available 8/82*)   P 587, $2.84
"Right now we'd call Mrs. Huxley a dangerous rival to Agatha Christie."   *—Books*

Francis Iles

BEFORE THE FACT   P 517, $1.95
"Not many 'serious' novelists have produced character studies to compare with Iles's internally terrifying portrait of the murderer in *Before the Fact,* his masterpiece and a work truly deserving the appellation of unique and beyond price."   *—Howard Haycraft*

MALICE AFORETHOUGHT   P 532, $1.95
"It is a long time since I have read anything so good as *Malice Aforethought,* with its cynical humour, acute criminology, plausible detail and rapid movement. It makes you hug yourself with pleasure."
—H. C. Harwood, Saturday Review

Michael Innes

DEATH BY WATER   P 574, $2.40
"The amount of ironic social criticism and deft characterization of scenes and people would serve another author for six books."
—Jacques Barzun and Wendell Hertig Taylor

HARE SITTING UP (*available 9/82*)   P 590, $2.84
"There is hardly anyone (in mysteries or mainstream) more exquisitely literate, allusive and Jamesian—and hardly anyone with a firmer sense of melodramatic plot or a more vigorous gift of storytelling."
—Anthony Boucher, The New York Times

THE LONG FAREWELL   P 575, $2.40
"A model of the deft, classic detective story, told in the most wittily diverting prose."   *—The New York Times*

THE MAN FROM THE SEA (*available 9/82*)   P 591, $2.84
"The pace is brisk, the adventures exciting and excitingly told, and above all he keeps to the very end the interesting ambiguity of the man from the sea."   *—New Statesman*

Michael Innes (cont'd)

THE SECRET VANGUARD   P 584, $2.84

"Innes . . . has mastered the art of swift, exciting and well-organized narrative."
                                                    —*The New York Times*

Mary Kelly

THE SPOILT KILL   P 565, $2.40

"Mary Kelly is a new Dorothy Sayers. . . . [An] exciting new novel."
                                                    —*Evening News*

Lange Lewis

THE BIRTHDAY MURDER   P 518, $1.95

"Almost perfect in its playlike purity and delightful prose."
                                        —*Jacques Barzun and Wendell Hertig Taylor*

Allan MacKinnon

HOUSE OF DARKNESS   P 582, $2.84

"His best . . . a perfect compendium."
                        —*Jacques Barzun & Wendell Hertig Taylor, A Catalogue of Crime*

Arthur Maling

LUCKY DEVIL   P 482, $1.95

"The plot unravels at a fast clip, the writing is breezy and Maling's approach is as fresh as today's stockmarket quotes."
                                                    —*Louisville Courier Journal*

RIPOFF   P 483, $1.95

"A swiftly paced story of today's big business is larded with intrigue as a Ralph Nader-type investigates an insurance scandal and is soon on the run from a hired gun and his brother. . . . Engrossing and credible."
                                                    —*Booklist*

SCHROEDER'S GAME   P 484, $1.95

"As the title indicates, this Schroeder is up to something, and the unravelling of his game is a diverting and sufficiently blood-soaked entertainment."
                                                    —*The New Yorker*

Austin Ripley

MINUTE MYSTERIES   P 387, $2.50

More than one hundred of the world's shortest detective stories. Only one possible solution to each case!

Thomas Sterling

THE EVIL OF THE DAY   P 529, $2.50
"Prose as witty and subtle as it is sharp and clear...characters unconventionally conceived and richly bodied forth.... In short, a novel to be treasured."   —Anthony Boucher, *The New York Times*

Julian Symons

THE BELTING INHERITANCE   P 468, $1.95
"A superb whodunit in the best tradition of the detective story."
                    —August Derleth, *Madison Capital Times*

BLAND BEGINNING   P 469, $1.95
"Mr. Symons displays a deft storytelling skill, a quiet and literate wit, a nice feeling for character, and detectival ingenuity of a high order."
                    —Anthony Boucher, *The New York Times*

BOGUE'S FORTUNE   P 481, $1.95
"There's a touch of the old sardonic humour, and more than a touch of style."   —*The Spectator*

THE BROKEN PENNY   P 480, $1.95
"The most exciting, astonishing and believable spy story to appear in years."   —Anthony Boucher, *The New York Times Book Review*

THE COLOR OF MURDER   P 461, $1.95
"A singularly unostentatious and memorably brilliant detective story."
                    —*New York Herald Tribune Book Review*

THE 31ST OF FEBRUARY   P 460, $1.95
"Nobody has painted a more gruesome picture of the advertising business since Dorothy Sayers wrote 'Murder Must Advertise', and very few people have written a more entertaining or dramatic mystery story."
                    —*The New Yorker*

Dorothy Stockbridge Tillet
(John Stephen Strange)

THE MAN WHO KILLED FORTESCUE   P 536, $2.25
"Better than average."   —*Saturday Review of Literature*

Simon Troy

THE ROAD TO RHUINE   P 583, $2.84
"Unusual and agreeably told."   —*San Francisco Chronicle*

Simon Troy (cont'd)

SWIFT TO ITS CLOSE   P 546, $2.40
"A nicely literate British mystery . . . the atmosphere and the plot are exceptionally well wrought, the dialogue excellent."   —*Best Sellers*

Henry Wade

THE DUKE OF YORK'S STEPS (*available 8/82*)   P 588, $2.84
"A classic of the golden age."
   —Jacques Barzun & Wendell Hertig Taylor, *A Catalogue of Crime*

A DYING FALL   P 543, $2.50
"One of those expert British suspense jobs . . . it crackles with undercurrents of blackmail, violent passion and murder. Topnotch in its class."
                    —*Time*

THE HANGING CAPTAIN   P 548, $2.50
"This is a detective story for connoisseurs, for those who value clear thinking and good writing above mere ingenuity and easy thrills."
                    —*Times Literary Supplement*

Hillary Waugh

LAST SEEN WEARING . . .   P 552, $2.40
"A brilliant tour de force."   —*Julian Symons*

THE MISSING MAN   P 553, $2.40
"The quiet detailed police work of Chief Fred C. Fellows, Stockford, Conn., is at its best in *The Missing Man* . . . one of the Chief's toughest cases and one of the best handled."
                —Anthony Boucher, *The New York Times Book Review*

Henry Kitchell Webster

WHO IS THE NEXT?   P 539, $2.25
"A double murder, private-plane piloting, a neat impersonation, and a delicate courtship are adroitly combined by a writer who knows how to use the language."   —Jacques Barzun and Wendell Hertig Taylor

Anna Mary Wells

MURDERER'S CHOICE   P 534, $2.50
"Good writing, ample action, and excellent character work."
                    —*Saturday Review of Literature*

Anna Mary Wells (cont'd)

A TALENT FOR MURDER   P 535, $2.25
"The discovery of the villain is a decided shock."   —*Books*

Edward Young

THE FIFTH PASSENGER   P 544, $2.25
"Clever and adroit . . . excellent thriller . . ."   —*Library Journal*

If you enjoyed this book you'll want to know about
THE PERENNIAL LIBRARY MYSTERY SERIES
Buy them at your local bookstore or use this coupon for ordering:

Qty	P number	Price

	postage and handling charge	$1.00
_____ book(s) @ $0.25		_____
	TOTAL	

Prices contained in this coupon are Harper & Row invoice prices only.
They are subject to change without notice, and in no way reflect the prices at
which these books may be sold by other suppliers.

**HARPER & ROW, Mail Order Dept. #PMS, 10 East 53rd St., New
York, N.Y. 10022.**
Please send me the books I have checked above. I am enclosing $_____
which includes a postage and handling charge of $1.00 for the first book and
25¢ for each additional book. Send check or money order. No cash or
C.O.D.s please

Name_____

Address_____

City_____ State_____ Zip_____
Please allow 4 weeks for delivery. USA only. This offer expires 6/30/83.
Please add applicable sales tax.